THE OTHER JUDAS
CATALUNYA HARDCORE

OLIVER J. PETRY

"The Other Judas" is invoked above all in difficult and hopeless situations.

Believers who implore the apostle for help often report miracles.

Saint Jude Thaddeus is considered the patron saint of impossible causes and a great helper in difficult situations.

Jean Sarre, an expert and former legionnaire, uncovers criminal activities in northern Spain.

He quickly finds himself caught up in a vicious circle of greed, power, sex, and violence.

But the antihero knows from experience that heavenly assistance can't hurt.

The other Judas

CATALUNYA HARDCORE

by Oliver J. Petry

In loving memory of Elke and Hanna

1st edition, 2025
© 2025 Oliver J. Petry
All rights reserved.

This novel is pure fiction. Any similarities or names that may appear in this work are purely coincidental and unintentional.
Certain passages may be triggering for readers who have experienced sexual violence or abuse.

for my English-speaking friends
1st edition – American first edition, June 2025
Contact: Petry@email.de
© Cover, pictures, title, and text – Oliver J. Petry – all rights reserved.

Publisher:
BoD · Books on Demand GmbH, Überseering 33, 22297 Hamburg, bod@bod.de
Print:
Libri Plureos GmbH, Friedensallee 273, 22763 Hamburg

ISBN: 978-3-8192-6715-4

Fire investigator and former legionnaire Jean Sarre is called to the scene of an accident and discovers that the wrecked car was not involved in an accident at all, but was the target of an arson attack. This is the beginning of an investigation that takes on ever greater proportions. The involvement of a not always very diligent detective, a corrupt building contractor, several petty criminals, an unscrupulous doctor, and some gorgeous women makes for an explosive mix!

About the author:
Oliver J. Petry was born in Saarbrücken in 1965 and has remained loyal to his Saarland homeland to this day. The automotive test engineer and expert runs a small testing center in northern Saarland. His exciting short stories and novels are influenced by his love of technology, music, nature, animals, and art.

Prologue

In the pale yellow spotlight, the winding road between Roses and Cadaqués seemed somehow unreal but largely safe. No wonder, since in the dark it was difficult to see that in places the road dropped almost 230 feet. The driver of the large silver limousine was in a better mood than he had been in a long time, and melodic rock music was playing on the car radio. He had finally made it. Gerard now had enough money to settle down for good. All he had to do now was pick up his lover and get out of Spain.
"Somehow damn romantic, almost like Shakespeare!" he thought to himself with a grin and turned up the volume of »Liquid Love« a notch.
Gerard Brieaux was a man in his late thirties who often sent women into raptures. The well-groomed, southern European type with shoulder-length jet-black hair epitomized the "Latin lover" cliché and was often told how much he looked like the actor Antonio Banderas. Without this asset, Gerard would have had a very difficult time in recent years. His work as an investigative journalist wasn't working out as he had hoped. Moreover, there wasn't much money to be made as a photographer.
Two years ago, he had been scraping by as a celebrity photographer.
But then he made a serious mistake that disqualified him from this profession as well.

At the time, he was following a Hollywood diva in Barcelona. Foolishly, it turned out to be a movie double who led him a merry dance. It didn't take long before he was the target of ridicule and scorn. After the shitstorm on the internet had subsided, Gerard had lost this career prospect and, moreover, had no more income. That's why he couldn't help but let a few wealthy ladies maintain him from time to time. After all, his life, or rather his exclusive lifestyle, had to be maintained. Gerard had never enjoyed having a regular job. Even as a child, he had his head in the clouds and created his own glamorous dream world. Let the others slave away. He was definitely too good for that. Since fine feathers make fine birds, as we all know, and the athletically ambitious Gerard rarely had any money in his pocket, he let well-off and unsatisfied women dress him so that they could then undress him again. Pretending to be in love had never really bothered him. He was only too happy to be fed. After all, he paid back in kind, so to speak. But when he met this dark-haired beauty at a charity party, it was supposed to be over. Besides, with her help, he had caught the big fish.

Gerard suddenly began to shiver and turned the heating up two notches. That damn electric sunroof hadn't closed properly for a few days. "Never mind," he thought, since he only needed the old BMW tonight. Everything would be fine, because he and his sweetheart would be in the Caribbean tomorrow anyway.

Out of nowhere, a single headlight suddenly appeared behind his car. Gerard was blinded for a moment by the glare in his rearview mirror and frantically flipped it up. Seconds later, someone started to pass him. "What a madman, and with these sharp curves," he thought as a motorcycle roared past him. Gerard was still annoyed about the reckless overtaking maneuver when he suddenly saw the bike standing unattended at the side of the road. Just before a dangerous left turn, he began to brake and wondered whether he should back up. At that moment, Gerard saw a person running toward him with something flickering in their hands. Brieaux was startled and wanted to stop, but then, out of nowhere, something bright flew into his car. Within milliseconds, the interior of the car was on fire and blood was running down his forehead. Something had cut him. Warm blood blurred his vision. There was fire everywhere. The last thing Gerard could think was, "He should never have come back!" The large silver sedan crashed through the guardrail, burst into flames, rolled over, and plunged unstoppably into the rocky, black depths.

CHAPTER 1: *Tramuntana*

"Damn Tramuntana, I feel like I've been sandblasted," thought Jean as he placed a large metal bowl of fresh water in front of the lean but muscular dog. The Doberman immediately began lapping up the cool water noisily.

With a broad smile, the pale man opened an ice-cold can of San Miguel. "I really needed that," he thought as he took big gulps of the Spanish beer. Then he threw open the balcony door. Unlike the front of the house, the veranda seemed largely sheltered from the wind.

Outside the pool, a large calf bone lay in the afternoon sun. "Looks kind of strange," he mused, but at the same time his dog already had the chunky bone in its mouth.

"Boy, where have you been hiding that thing all this time? Come back into the shade quickly!" The dog immediately dropped his toy. Then he lay down in front of Jean and waited for a new command. Maybe he was just adoring the human. Arthos loved his master. After all, the man had rescued him from extremely poor conditions. Not so long ago, the Doberman male, who had spent his youth on a chain, was considered unadoptable. It was only by chance that the two came together about two years ago, and they had been inseparable ever since.

After spreading out a Catalan daily newspaper in front of him, Jean began to read. Two minutes later, he put it down in annoyance and went to the pool. It was simply too hot to concentrate on any business news. Besides, he was thinking about his life so far. The man looked at his dog and suddenly had the same long face.

He was born almost 48 years ago in a small village near the French border. Although he had somehow managed his life so far, he had rarely been truly satisfied. It was high time to "take a break" again. Jean Sarre had worked almost everywhere, including some time in rainy Germany. Among other things, he had been an expert in fire damage.

You earned a reasonable salary and had a more or less easy job. However, the economic and social situation in your old home country was deteriorating rapidly. In addition, more and more people were simply being made redundant so that share prices and dividends could continue to rise. Here in northern Spain, you could do the same job for an insurance company. At least you liked the climate and the Mediterranean lifestyle of the people much better.

Jean Sarre was of medium height, middle age, and moderately good-looking. He often felt mediocre. That was what bothered him most about himself at the moment. But ultimately, he could be satisfied with his current life. At least that's what he kept telling himself.

Years ago, he had imagined his life would be different; classic... with a wife, children... well, at least he had a dog. And he could feel responsible for him, at least.

With temperatures still above 86 degrees in the shade, he was glad to have rented a house with a small outdoor pool. He was still enjoying this luxury to the fullest.

Suddenly, his cell phone rang. The black and brown dog jumped up and barked. Cursing under his breath, he climbed out of the pool, dripping wet, and picked up the phone with his still wet hands ..."Sarre!"

"Hola Señor Sarre," said a bright female voice on the other end. 'Perdón for disturbing you on a Sunday ... And I see you have 14 days' vacation starting the day after tomorrow. I wish I did. Anyway ... Can you head straight to Cadaqués first thing tomorrow morning? Last night, a car from GI 614 crashed into a ravine there. You know the winding road ... Please examine the vehicle; it's completely burned out ... The driver is dead, by the way. It's terrible ... a Frenchman, a photographer ... You'll drive there ... the police, Señor Inspector Ruiz ... he'll be in touch with you ... Hasta luego y Gracias!"

After assuring the clerk that he would be there at around 8:00 a.m. the next morning, Sarre placed his wet smartphone on the white table. He grabbed a large, dark blue bath towel and began to dry himself off, thinking about his current workload. At the moment, he couldn't complain about a lack of work. He had only been back in the country for a few months and was busy with work almost every day. But on weekends, he took the time to explore the area with Arthos and improve his language skills. He also loved music more than anything else. When he wasn't listening to well-made rock music, he picked up his acoustic guitar. He would strum a few chords or even try his hand at a solo.

Jean went into the house, picked up the newspaper, and threw it with gusto into the floor-standing file holder, also known as the wastebasket. Next, he picked up his old Gibson J45. He played a few chords in succession on the acoustic guitar. "Am, Em, Am, G, C, F, Em, Am, G, F, Em, Am."

It reminded him of a spaghetti western in which an aging gunslinger, played by Henry Fonda, had to take on a superior force known as the "Wild Bunch." The brilliant Ennio Morricone had covered Richard Wagner's "Ride of the Valkyries" and even freshened it up with car horns. The whole thing was downright epic!

He played the theme three or four times. But when Arthos whined softly, he put his beloved instrument back in its battered case.

"Hahaha ... All right, Okay boy! I'll stop strumming, Arthos!"

Jean laughed as he closed the guitar case.

The dog watched Jean with interest and then began to yawn profusely. The expert couldn't help but smile at his unmusical Doberman, although the dog's yawning could of course also be a signal of appeasement.

However, Jean was now yawning too and felt a certain tiredness coming on. So he would have to go to bed earlier tonight after all. Best right after dinner. After all, he had to be reasonably fit tomorrow.

About twelve miles away, at about the same time, Juan Falgas was also swimming in his pool. The difference was that this swimming pool was more the size of a public outdoor pool. It was simply huge and you could swim laps wonderfully. The well-trained man, almost 58 years old, stepped lightly out of the water and flicked a switch.

It took no more than 30 seconds for one of his servants to run down the steps to the pool with a large bath towel. As soon as the butler had handed the towel to his "jefe," he had to listen to a few insults.

"Oye cabrón, where's my Rioja and my Cohibas? You idiots should know the days of the week by now. Today is Sunday, and what are you wannabe servants supposed to bring me on a Sunday evening? Mierda, vete tonto, now run and fetch it before I kick your lame ass!"

After the frightened servant had climbed the stairs to the main house again, amid a torrent of abuse, the aggression turned to the pretty dark-haired woman on the other side of the pool.

"It's all your fault, Mercedes! How do you pick our staff? You're just as weak as your father! All you can do is look pretty!"

The extremely pretty woman showed no reaction. She knew that this would get her nowhere with her sometimes choleric husband. So she swallowed and tried to think of better days.

Her Juanito used to be completely different. Nice, polite, and always respectful toward others. Her father had found his "dream son-in-law" in him, and it wasn't long before the old patriarch signed over the entire company to him.

Today, Mercedes Falgas, née Leon, knew that love really could be blind. She just wanted to get away.

Besides, she was even sadder than usual because she was expecting a call from a man who could free her from her constant fear. But the call was long overdue.

During his lifetime, her father Pedro Leon saw only the good in people. After making a fortune as a first-time entrepreneur in the construction industry, he supported all kinds of charitable organizations. He built small hospitals, nursing homes, and schools, especially in the neighboring Pyrenees, to provide basic mental and medical care for the inhabitants.

He himself came from one of these small, isolated mountain farming villages and knew the locals and their problems only too well. But then, just under two years ago, Pedro Leon suffered a sudden and severe heart attack, which the "big property tycoon" did not survive.

On Monday morning, around 5:30 a.m., a still tired Jean and his large Doberman were already out and about on the deserted beach. Here in Empuriabrava, dogs were officially not allowed on the beach or on any green spaces. Prohibition signs with the words "No Perros" (No Dogs) were now posted everywhere. Jean Sarre wondered where all the dogs in town were supposed to go.

Sure, who wants to step in dog poop all the time? But a responsible dog owner always carries a plastic bag to dispose of their pet's waste in a suitable place.

Despite the general ban, Sarre knew where the "dog spots" were. After all, he had spent a lot of his free time in the Bay of Roses. Jean and, most likely, Arthos were particularly fond of the wild beach between the mouth of the Muga River and the fishing village of San Pere de Pescador.

Behind it lay the Aiguamolls bird sanctuary.

When you walked for miles on the fine-grained sand there, you really didn't feel like you were in an area overrun by tourists. Thankfully, over the years, the Spanish had also realized that nature conservation and species protection were important tasks that ultimately shaped the face of the Costa Brava, the "wild coast."

This area was more or less new to the five-year-old male dog. So he stopped more often than usual to sniff the air. His owner made sure he didn't do anything stupid, but even dogs need to "read the paper."

After Jean had breakfast on his porch—well, you couldn't exactly call the double cortado and Lucky Strike 'breakfast'—he took care of Arthos. "Okay, buddy. You stay right here and leave the leather couch alone!" Jean couldn't help but grin when the dog growled softly, as if to say, "You can't do anything here!"

Jean grabbed his work gear and drove his old SUV out of the driveway.

Then he got out again to lock the large iron gate. It was actually relatively unnecessary to lock it because Arthos was standing guard.

Well, Jean simply loved double security measures. Perhaps that was one of the reasons for his secure but also dull and currently unspectacular life.

Several years ago, he wanted, or rather had to, leave uncomfortable Germany. At that time, however, it would have been much riskier for him to settle in a foreign country. But now he had planned his "exit" and done it. Probably, though, other factors had given him the final push.

Whatever the case, Jean Sarre had lost the only person he could really talk to about anything almost two years ago. His long-time girlfriend had suddenly become terminally ill, and within a few weeks, pancreatic cancer had won.

He often thought back to the wonderful and far too short time he had spent with Inga, a Swedish woman. He usually lit one cigarette after another defiantly and lost in thought.

Soon he had left urbanization behind him on his way to the hinterland. "It's very quiet here. It would be nice if everything wasn't so burnt," he thought to himself, and the expert knew, of course, that it wasn't naive tourists who were behind it, but the construction mafia. Unscrupulous profiteers who put people in danger and deliberately destroyed nature just to get cheap building land.

A name that often came up in this context was "Falgas," but these were only unconfirmed rumors.

When he arrived at the scene of the accident, the police and a tow truck were already there.

He parked his SUV behind the recovery vehicle, but before he could get out, a blond man came up to him, fuming with rage.

"You there, get out of here! This is a police operation. Go away! Journalists are not allowed here, take your photos somewhere else!"

"Hold on a minute, I'm Jean Sarre, the Estrella Insurance assessor, not some newspaper hack!" Jean replied to the man in front of him.

Suddenly, the policeman with the stringy hair and huge nose became meek, and the annoyed Jean realized that the whole thing was very embarrassing for the law enforcement officer.

"Oh, I'm sorry, Señor Sarre, I thought you were one of those 'newspaper hacks'. I'm Inspector Carlos Ruiz and I thought you wouldn't be coming to the workshop in Figueres until later.

Besides, I wasn't expecting you so early.

As you can see, we're recovering the burned-out BMW 7 Series. The dead Frenchman, or rather what's left of him, has been at the Girona coroner's office since Sunday morning," said the burly man almost quietly, and Jean's pulse rate slowly returned to normal.

In the meantime, a few gawkers had gathered to watch the recovery with euphoria.

Rubbernecks stopped behind the recovery vehicle and looked down into the ravine through binoculars and cameras. Jean Sarre gave Carlos Ruiz a nod, and the inspector shouted out some instructions.

The police immediately cordoned off half the street. Then they began to disperse the onlookers with force.

Jean wanted to light a cigarette and searched desperately for a lighter in his Bermuda shorts.

The inspector pulled a brass storm lighter from his pants pocket and handed it to him. "Take it and keep it, I've just quit smoking. You know, -fumar puede matar-," Carlos Ruiz remarked with a grin.

Jean smiled, thanked him politely, and after a brief briefing, the two set off on the arduous journey to the scene of the accident.

The expert was glad to have arrived just in time before a rescue team could attach heavy ropes to the wrecked car.

The burnt-out wreck lay about 55 yards below the bend in the road, between two rocks, on its roof. The driver of the formerly silver BMW had apparently lost control of his car in a left-hand bend. The car must have shot through the guardrail, plunged into the ravine, rolled over several times, and then burned out.

After Jean Sarre had examined the car, taken photos for evidence, and climbed back up the mountain, he began to feel a certain hunger. No wonder, considering the "opulent meal" he had prepared for himself that morning.

He was also worried about Arthos and the new leather couch. So he drove home pretty quickly.

After a typical single person's meal consisting of a reheated pizza that was just past its expiration date, he took care of his homework. First, he transferred the digital photos to his laptop. Then he called the auto repair shop to make a second appointment to have the car inspected on the lift.

The photos had turned out well, but he noticed a bright spot on one of them that he couldn't quite explain. Something was reflecting the sun's rays. He enlarged the image but still couldn't make out what it was. Maybe a tin, a coin, or something similar? Slowly but surely, his curiosity got the better of him.

Once again, Jean thought of the old spaghetti western. Henry Fonda was only able to defeat the galloping villains because the silver stars on their saddlebags reflected the sun. The bags contained sticks of dynamite, of all things. Fonda, alias Jack Beauregard, only had to aim at the flashes of light to pulverize the "Wild Bunch." Now he remembered the title of the film. A Sergio Leone western from 1973, which was released in theaters under the name "My Name is Nobody." Of course, the sly Terence Hill, alias Nobody, had a starring role in the film. Jean liked these old "spaghetti westerns."

A good two hours later, he set off again for the scene of the accident. He parked his car in a nearby parking bay, climbed over the battered guardrail, and scrambled laboriously down the slope. By the time he reached the bottom, he was completely drenched in sweat. No wonder, because at around 1:00 p.m., the sun was beating down mercilessly once again.

CHAPTER 2: *The discovery and the opportunities*

It took a while, but he found what he was looking for. Beneath a rock lay a brown suede bag with chrome clasps. He quickly stuffed it into his backpack and started back down the slope.

When he looked up at the mountain, he saw that a car was parked behind his. Sarre could easily see that it was a police car.

With a strange feeling in his stomach and lots of excuses in his head, he started the climb.

But when he reached the top, his car was standing there all alone. Jean felt somehow guilty. He wondered if it wouldn't be better to take the bag to the police station right away. On the other hand, he could always do that later. So the expert placed it under the driver's seat of his SUV and drove off to do some shopping.

In the afternoon, Jean sat on his porch with the leather bag on the white plastic table in front of him. "Let's see what's inside; I feel like a little boy on Christmas Eve," he thought to himself, while Arthos yawned quietly. When he emptied the bag, however, he was quite disappointed. The only interesting thing was a small key. It must have belonged to a locker. Based on a crumpled gas station receipt, he guessed it was from the Barcelona airport.

He also found a brochure for a construction company. And a note with a phone number and the initials "MF."
Should he take the bag to Police Inspector Ruiz in the morning? That would probably be best! But he could also drive to the airport tomorrow. Just to see if his guess was right. He thought and thought. What could the dead Frenchman have left behind that was so valuable? But Jean had become too curious. Besides, he had business to attend to in Barcelona anyway.

Two years earlier, Juan Falgas was already the largest construction contractor in the region. However, at least among the common people, he was not nearly as respected as his late father-in-law. No wonder, because since Pedro Leon's death, Juan had completely changed his life, both privately and professionally. He made a name for himself in the construction business in no time. And when people today spoke reverently about the kind-hearted "Don Pedro," they whispered only quietly about the distinguished but devious Juan.
There were many stories about the "construction magnate" Falgas and his dubious business dealings, but everything was said behind closed doors. He was said to have connections to the Spanish royal family, to tolerate no dissent, and that anyone who got in his way would suffer.
There was a constant buzz of rumors surrounding Juan Falgas.

Of course, there was also a lot of envy. His employees and workers earned above the standard wage, but in return they had to put up with his mood swings.

At least some of them did, because Falgas had also brought in some Colombian workers in the past.

Shortly before the illegal immigrants were discovered, Juan received a tip from a good friend in the public prosecutor's office.

Now the nursing homes, high up in the inaccessible mountains, were finally paying off. No one would suspect the cheap laborers there. However, the Colombians were now costing him money every day, and he was constantly thinking about what to do with the isolated workers.

About three weeks after the "evacuation," he had a brilliant idea, of all places, at the Peralada golf club. His old school friend, District Attorney Rodriguez, was once again complaining to him about his troubles. His son Franco Junior was suffering from a serious kidney disease and, despite dialysis treatment, had no chance of survival without a donor.

"What would you do if I got a new kidney for your son?"

The prosecutor was taken aback. "How are you going to do that? You can't get one anywhere in Spain at the moment!"

"One good turn deserves another, Franco! You gave me a tip, now it's my turn to do you a favor!"

"Get me all the medical records, I'll take care of the rest."

The next morning, right after breakfast, Juan Falgas drove his Porsche Cabriolet into the mountains. He had actually considered contacting the chief physician beforehand. But the matter was simply too sensitive to be dealt with over the phone.

When he arrived in Vidasacra around noon, he was already quite irritated.

Even the fast Porsche was useless on the narrow, pothole-ridden roads. He had managed to overtake a few trucks, but Juan and his brand-new 911 Turbo could have done without that "thrill."

Besides, he couldn't get the old woman out of his head. About halfway there, she was standing there, dressed all in black, waving at him from the side of the road. Apparently, the frail old lady wanted to hitchhike because she suddenly staggered onto the road.

Juan honked wildly, swerved to avoid the woman, and said goodbye rather rudely with his middle finger extended.

He almost ruined one of his expensive Cup rims in the evasive maneuver.

Falgas would never have picked up that old hag. His sports car was definitely too chic for that. He only allowed women who were well past menopause to sit on the leather seats of his Porsche.

Juan Falgas was an utterly unempathetic upstart who would have betrayed and sold his own mother. And that wasn't all, for sure!

Back then, once Juan was sure he was his father-in-law's favorite, he came up with a sneaky plan. As soon as the old patriarch signed over his company, he had to leave, and fast.

After all, it wasn't that unusual for people to die shortly after retiring. A friend gave Juan a great idea. In a botanical garden, Falgas found what he was looking for: the "Blue Monkshood". Aconite, the main active ingredient found in all parts of the plant, was already popular with assassins in the Middle Ages. The root tubers of monkshood are particularly poisonous. Even when dried, the lethal dose for an adult is only one to two grams. Juan, the "dream son-in-law," invited his father-in-law to a golf match in Peralada. After letting Don Pedro beat him, the two men wanted to celebrate the beautiful day a little longer. Pedro Leon was generous, and they ate and drank without worrying about money. Half an hour after the first drink, Don Pedro was dead.

"At this time of day, I'm sure to find the fat Dr. Kremer doing his favorite thing," thought the building contractor, and made his way to the hospital cafeteria.

Dr. Eugenio Kremer was just tucking into his second helping when Falgas greeted him with a smile. "Hola Doctor, you look well. I have something important to discuss with you. Let's go to your office, where we'll have some peace and quiet. Come on!"

Doc Kremer was a tall, pale man who weighed almost 440 pounds. He looked a bit like an unkempt teddy bear. His small, dark button eyes, which looked huge behind his thick black horn-rimmed glasses, reinforced this impression.

The doctor didn't like being disturbed while he was eating. But after all, the uninvited guest was his financial backer. So a forced smile appeared on his thick lips.

"Ah, my friend, dear Señor Falgas, how can I help you … just spit it out," replied the doctor in a high falsetto voice that didn't suit the big man at all.

After Falgas had explained his plan to the doctor, there was silence in the well-air-conditioned room for a while.

"Oh really? A kidney transplant and an unwilling donor. I need a drink first... Would you like one?" Juan Falgas knew that Doctor Kremer could pull it off. After all, the only reason he was in this deserted Pyrenean village was because no one knew him here. Just five years ago, he had been working as a surgeon in Madrid until the poison cabinet affair came to light. All he wanted to do at the time was "separate" from his girlfriend.

"No, I have to drive back, and you shouldn't drink anything either. At least nothing alcoholic. Examine our Colombians as quickly as possible, tell them something, and get everything started.

When you have the donor, don't call me, just send me a text message. Write 'kidney' and I'll have the sick boy brought to you. And don't let this hurt you, Doc!"

Two weeks later, the whole thing was over. The doctor was a few euros richer and the prosecutor's son finally had the kidney he had been longing for. The chances were good that he would be able to live on.

Everything went well. Dr. Kremer was extremely satisfied with himself and his work. So satisfied that he sent Juan Falgas an offer via text message. "Kidney harvest excellent. More interested parties wanted!"

Falgas was cold-hearted enough to accept. Now, at last, the isolated cheap laborers were bringing him good money, albeit in a different way than he had imagined. In just a few months, with the help of Dr. Eugenio Kremer, the internet, and, last but not least, "his isolated ones," he was able to build up a brisk organ trade. The demand for various organs rose so rapidly that Falgas had to increase his supply. So he hired more workers "for exploitation" through a Colombian friend. The illegal workers were smuggled into the country and first examined by Dr. Kremer. They were then told that they would have to spend some time in quarantine before they could earn big money.

The Colombian middleman was now earning significantly more and never asked any questions. The only thing that gave Juan Falgas some jitters was the thought of what Dr. Kremer might be doing with the human remains. However, the doctor was responsible for disposing of the bodies. After all, it was his business, and he had the necessary expertise.

The organ trade flourished, and it took about two years before Juan Falgas was blackmailed. He would probably have to pay, but he would also make sure that the photographer disappeared from his Mercedes's life.

The trip to Barcelona went smoothly. Jean Sarre was fairly familiar with the Catalan capital and made good progress on his motorcycle even during rush hour.

After completing his business errands (he had to stop by his employer's headquarters briefly), he made his way to the airport. By car, Jean would certainly have taken almost twice as long on Tuesday morning. What's more, he had no trouble finding a parking space with his "Triumph". However, his leather suit wasn't particularly suitable for summer, and the Spanish asphalt radiated incredible heat in the midday sun. After parking his three-cylinder bike right at the entrance to the imposing airport building, Jean entered the lobby, sweaty and with his helmet and backpack in hand. Inside, the air was twenty degrees cooler than outside and it felt like being "flash frozen." No sooner had Jean entered than he was almost knocked over by a family of five with their luggage. At least the father apologized to Jean. After the suitcases and travel accessories had been stowed away on the trolley, the expert tried to get an overview of the situation. Not so easy with all the people around. Jean felt like he was in a beehive. Or perhaps a mass panic was a better comparison.

After a while, he finally found the room with the lockers. "635," he thought aloud, the locker had to be there somewhere. It took him a full three minutes to find it. Then he searched the inside pocket of his motorcycle jacket for the small key. After a long search, he found it and compared the numbers again. Jean realized that he was becoming quite panicked while searching. He sat down on a wooden bench to calm himself. The expert was just about to light a cigarette when a security guard drew his attention to a metal sign. "Prohibido a fumar" (No smoking) it said, and Sarre cursed himself in that moment. The last thing he needed now was unnecessary attention. So he smiled apologetically at the security guard and demonstratively put the cigarettes away. After the security guard had walked away with a stern expression and a raised index finger, Jean got up from the old wooden bench and went back to the locker.

With trembling hands, he put the small key in the lock. He was actually quite surprised that it fit.

"So I got the combination right after all," thought Jean," let's see what's inside."

He opened the safe, looked inside, and then broke out in a cold sweat.

Inside the locker was a small metal box full of money, a CD, two expired airline tickets, several receipts, and a pistol with two loaded magazines.

"Bull's-eye," thought Sarre. With adrenaline pumping through his veins, he quickly shoved the items into his backpack and left, having to pull himself together to appear halfway inconspicuous.

As he left the well-air-conditioned airport building and braced himself for another physical temperature shock, he noticed a matte black Ducati next to his Triumph motorbike. This Italian motorcycle was available in black, but this one looked as if it had been spray-painted.

"Hideous," he mused, 'and on a new motorcycle.' The Duc also had a modified cockpit. He thought he could make out some kind of navigation system. But Jean had neither the time nor the nerves to look at the technical features of someone else's motorcycle. So he got on his English lady and drove off. On the way back, Sarre thought a few times about stopping somewhere to take another look at "his prize." But for safety reasons, he quickly dismissed the idea.

For a moment, the expert had the feeling he was being followed. But at the same time, he smiled at himself and his emerging paranoia.

It was logical that Jean would develop such feelings; after all, he was driving around with several thousand euros.

Suddenly, a black motorcycle overtook him. He was pretty sure it was the matte black Ducati 900 Monster that was parked next to his Speed Triple at the airport.

As soon as the rider, dressed entirely in black, was level with him, he lifted his Ducati onto its rear wheel. Jean wasn't going to be provoked by such a "wheelie." The show-off was probably hoping for a little race. But the expert wasn't going to give the hothead the satisfaction.

Besides, Jean Sarre had become calmer over the years.

He knew only too well how easy it was to skid on the sandy roads here.

When the expert arrived home, his cell phone showed two missed calls and a text message. The inspector wanted to know what he had found out about the burned-out BMW.

"Great!" thought Jean, who had completely forgotten about his workshop appointment in Figueres.

The expert hadn't even closed the front door behind him when the big Doberman rushed toward him. "Aaaarthos, nooooo, ... don't jump, sit!" Two seconds later, he was lying on his back on the floor of the hallway and was being licked thoroughly and according to all the rules of the art. It took a few minutes before he was able to curb the dog's exuberant joy at seeing him again. Then he took off his sweat-soaked motorcycle gear and had a cool drink.

Mineral water, of course, but Sarre decided to go to the pub around the corner that evening to celebrate his "find" a little. First, he had to take a closer look at the contents of the backpack. The pistol, a Glock 17, and the accompanying magazines interested him only marginally. The same went for the music CD, the receipts, and so on; he would take a closer look at those things later. But how much money was in the cash box, that was really important!

He started counting the bills. There were fifties, hundreds, two hundred, and now rare five hundred bills. Luckily, they were all used. Sarre counted exactly five hundred thousand euros. Amidst all the joy over the half million, he suddenly remembered that the front door was still open. A strange feeling came over him. He quickly went to the door and locked it. As he locked it, he heard a motorcycle drive by. The expert was familiar with the two-cylinder sound of the Desmo engine. It was the sound of a Ducati.

He quickly looked through one of the barred windows but couldn't see a motorcycle.

"Don't drive yourself crazy," Jean told himself. Then he thought about where he could best hide the money.

After doing so, he drove to Figueres. There, at the auto repair shop, he inspected the burned-out BMW. The expert was relatively certain that it was not an accident. Nevertheless, it looked like one. The garage owner just joked and made French jokes. "Hopefully you drive better than your compatriot, Monsieur Sarre!" he said to Jean with a broad smile. Jean grinned and didn't respond to the provocation. After the brief friendly banter, Jean Sarre looked at the wreck again and noticed the remains of a bottle neck in the back of the vehicle. There were some textile residues stuck to it. Sarre thought he knew what they were. To be sure, he examined the open sunroof of the BMW. Here, too, the expert found bottle glass shards. Now he was suddenly certain that it was not an accident.

"Shortly before his death, someone bought the Frenchman a cocktail. However, it wasn't served as a drink and didn't have a colorful umbrella in it!"

After securing the evidence, including taking more photos, he said goodbye to the garage owner and drove toward the police station in the afternoon sun.

Halfway there, Sarre turned around. He had to think quietly about how much he could tell Ruiz without attracting attention. Logically, the inspector couldn't know anything about the locker, let alone the half a million euros.

After all, Jean could use it to fill his almost empty pockets. Besides, the five hundred thousand euros would be a wonderful addition to his pension.

While Jean racked his brains, a good-looking blonde was fixing her hair. Freshly showered, she was getting ready to go out. The huge oval mirror on the bathroom door showed the woman in her late forties in all her beauty. People often mistook the tall, well-trained woman for a Scandinavian. She was born in Riga but grew up in Moscow. During the Warsaw Pact era, Elena Lokova had enjoyed an exceptional education at the expense of the USSR. When the Soviet Union collapsed in 1991, the talented woman was able to continue her work on a freelance basis due to the continuing demand. The difference was that she now earned ten times as much as a "cleaner."

Elena was currently thinking about how she could best wrap her "blind date" around her finger. However, she remained absolutely calm and composed, as she was well aware of her effect on the male sex.

When she came out of the bathroom, she took the black leather clothes off the chair. She then laid them out on the porch of her rented apartment to air out. There was a silver key on the small coffee table. She put it in her handbag.

There was a small red and silver symbol on the car key. Geometric, probably a cross between a circle and a triangle. Somehow like a deformed ellipse, on which six letters were strung together: "DUCATI."

The sun was just setting as Jean Sarre rode his English motorcycle to the Mossos d'Esquadra police station in Roses. He parked his blue Speed Triple near the entrance to the headquarters, right next to Inspector Ruiz's car. Once inside, he went to a kind of counter behind which sat a small, grumpy-looking police officer.

"Hola, my name is Sarre and I'd like to see Inspector Ruiz," Jean said to the man behind the counter. The policeman didn't react at first, but then he took two small headphones out of his ears.

"What do you want?" the law enforcement officer replied unfriendly.

But before Jean could repeat his request, Inspector Ruiz came around the corner with a coffee in his hand.

"Ah, Señor Sarre, great to see you, come into my office," said Carlos Ruiz loudly, waving his plastic cup.

"Hey Quitano!" Ruiz called to the small receptionist.

"Turn off the radio! Bring our visitor a coffee. And hurry up, hombre!"

The short policeman jumped up as if stung by a tarantula. It was a miracle he didn't salute.

"Would you like sugar, milk, or both in your coffee?" asked the inspector with a grin. Jean thanked him and replied that he would just like sugar. The inspector's office was anything but inviting. The old furniture was dark and dusty. A tiny window let neither daylight nor fresh air into the stuffy room. "Well then, let's get started, Mr. Expert. What have you found out?" said the policeman, running his fingers through his stringy blond hair. Jean looked at the big man and wondered which part of Spain he might come from. Somehow Carlos Ruiz looked more like a German farmer. Nothing against German farmers, but the man didn't fit the image of a Mediterranean at all. "You know, Señor Sarre, as far as I'm concerned, this matter is closed. My mother always told me never to drive faster than your guardian angel can fly! In the northwest of Spain, where I grew up, many tourists have crashed again this year. So write your report. Please send me a copy so I can file the accident away."

Now Sarre knew that the inspector was from the Basque Country and didn't really want to know anything more about the matter.

He was just about to speak when there was a tentative knock at the office door.

"Come in, Quitano, I hope the coffee's still hot for our guest!"

The little policeman politely handed Jean a plastic cup, avoiding eye contact.

Jean took a small sip. He wasn't really surprised that the coffee tasted awful. Then he started to speak again, but this time the inspector interrupted him.

"I hope you're enjoying our plastic coffee," said the policeman in an ironic tone. 'I'm sure the coffee at Estrella Insurance is better, but ours is made with love!' The smug grin disappeared instantly from the inspector's thick-nosed face when Jean threw the cup forcefully into the trash can.

Annoyed, he raised his voice.

"I don't care about your crappy coffee; this is about murder. This French photographer was murdered, get that into your bureaucratic skull!"

Then there was silence, at least for almost ten seconds. Then Carlos Ruiz spoke up. "What? Murder? What makes you think that?" whispered the inspector. Jean explained the situation to him, but with considerably less volume in his voice. Finally, he took a plastic bag out of his pocket. Jean demonstratively placed the neck of the bottle, along with the shards, on the solid office desk.

"Molotov cocktail (Molotov bomb), are you absolutely sure? I'll have our people examine the shards, you can count on that! But there's no need to raise your voice just because you don't like our coffee. Now I'll have to have the wall repainted. Perhaps you'd like a cognac? I have a good Osborne," said the inspector, rather meekly.

The big, burly man suddenly seemed very uncertain. No one had yelled at him like that in years, especially not in his own office.

"Have you found out anything else, Señor Sarre?" asked the inspector. 'No!' replied Jean. "But what have you found out about the dead photographer?"

"I'm not allowed to tell you that. You know how it is with ongoing investigations! All I can say is that the photographer, a certain Gerard Brieaux, also worked as a freelance journalist. He had a small rented apartment in Perpignan. If I notify our French colleagues and your assumption proves to be correct, we'll probably go looking for a motive together."

"Okay, Señor Inspector, you go ahead and investigate. I wish you the best of luck!" said Jean, annoyed at such narrow-mindedness. But above all, he was annoyed at the detective's lack of motivation. "Have a nice evening, Señor Sarre, and get home safely," replied Ruiz. Jean tried to smile politely as he got up. Before leaving the small, stuffy office, he nodded to Carlos Ruiz. "Disculpe, for the outburst,

Señor. Hasta luego!" The small, unfriendly police officer didn't even notice him as he left. He was engrossed in a magazine. He was also listening to 'Radio Catalan' again.

When Jean reached his motorcycle, he instinctively looked around. Maybe he was being paranoid, but he still had the feeling that someone was watching him. Now that he knew that the Frenchman, Gerard Brieaux, had been murdered, he couldn't expect to keep the stolen money without any problems.

Obviously, it wasn't the Frenchman's property. How could a photographer or journalist legally come by so much money? He had suspected from the beginning that something was fishy. Why would a photographer need a 9mm pistol? Only for self-defense. The man was probably terrified of someone. Jean was now annoyed that he had been so overwhelmed by the half a million. He should have looked at the other things in the damn locker first. But putting it off didn't mean it would be forgotten. So he made his way home again.

Despite his curiosity and the fact that his "doggie" was waiting for dinner, Jean drove back very cautiously and almost slowly. He wasn't exactly creeping along, but his defensive driving style certainly prevented him from crashing.

This very fact had saved his bones many times before. As a motorcyclist, you are largely unprotected. In a sense, your own body is the crumple zone.

What's more, the country roads between Roses and Figueres were quite accident-prone.

CHAPTER 3: *The collision and falling in love*

Forty meters ahead of him, the traffic light at the intersection turned red. Jean shifted down two gears in quick succession. He came to a stop at the stop line, relaxed his hands on the handlebars, and then there was a loud bang. Jean Sarre felt a violent blow to his back.

A black VW Golf had crashed into his Triumph. The Volkswagen pushed Sarre a good distance into the intersection. He tried to catch his motorcycle, but he couldn't because he couldn't get a grip on the wide handlebars due to the inertia. The motorcycle and he slid several meters across the dusty Catalan asphalt, sparks flying.

Thankfully, there was little traffic on the roads at the time, otherwise Jean would probably have been run over by cross traffic.

An elderly Dutchman reacted promptly and immediately switched on the hazard warning lights of his old Volvo when he saw the fallen motorcyclist lying in the middle of the intersection.

Cursing wildly, Jean Sarre tried to pick up his damaged Speed Triple. Out of the corner of his eye, he saw a tall, blonde woman running towards him from behind.

"Oh my God, ... oh my God, I didn't mean to! I didn't see you ... Are you hurt? Come on, I'll take you to the hospital," the blonde woman said to Jean.

"Can't you keep your eyes on the road? Learn to drive first!" Sarre replied angrily.

Jean Sarre didn't even look properly at the blonde woman. He was more interested in the condition of his motorcycle.

The crash pads he had recently installed had at least protected the cooling fins of the three-cylinder engine. But the rear, or rather the seat, had suffered badly. Logically, the turn signals had also been damaged.

"Great," Jean said loudly. "Estupendo, at least two thousand euros worth of damage."

"Here's my phone number. My name is Elena Lokova. I'll pay for the damage, of course. Come on, shouldn't I drive you to the hospital?"

"No, no, no, leave me alone! I'm fine," said Jean angrily. At the same time, he took the yellow piece of paper with the phone number on it.

In fact, he almost ripped the piece of paper out of her slender fingers. Only now did he take a closer look at the woman who had caused the accident.

Jean saw a pretty blonde in front of him and suddenly felt something like pity for the remorseful-looking woman.

"Well, shit happens, but you could have killed me!" he said to her. His expression even turned into an almost reassuring smile.

"As I said, I'm so sorry about the accident. Just tell me what I can do for you! I'll pay for the damage. Can I invite you to dinner? As a kind of additional compensation," said the attractive woman to Jean. He looked into her bright blue eyes.

Of course Jean didn't say no to that offer. If there was such a thing as 'love at first sight'... well, at least he had suddenly "fallen head over heels."

"Why not right now, in Empuriabrava? Do you know Port Grec? I was just about to go out for dinner anyway," he said to her. She smiled and agreed. They arranged that she would follow him. However, he had to take care of his dog first.

After all, although his Triumph was still roadworthy, neither the brakes nor the rear light were working. So she followed him, albeit at a considerable distance this time. After he had parked his wrecked bike and taken care of his dog, he at least freshened up a little. Then he got into her car.

"My first date in my new home," he thought. She had a smile that enchanted him. The food wasn't great, as it was rather salty overall. The cook was probably in love. But it didn't matter; Jean really blossomed in conversation with Elena. They talked about everything under the sun. After they agreed to drop the formalities, the "Lonesome Wolf" Sarre felt like he had known this woman for ages. They laughed a lot. But when Elena paid the bill as promised, Jean felt that this wonderful evening had gone by far too quickly. He looked a little sad.

"What are you looking at? Oh, sorry Jean, we're on first-name terms now. Shall we go for a drink somewhere?" Elena beamed at him.

There was little that could have stopped Jean. So the two of them had another carafe of red wine at `El Rastro`. At around half past two, it was slowly time to say goodbye.

When Elena kissed him tenderly on both cheeks and asked him if he wanted to come home with her, Jean felt like he had a thousand butterflies in his stomach.

There was no doubt about it, of course he wanted to. Jean Sarre had fallen head over heels in love with the beautiful woman. He had to admit to himself that he had rarely experienced such intense feelings, and not for a long time.

So the two drove to Elena's rented apartment in Roses. As soon as they entered the apartment, Elena took Jean by the hand. She gave him a tender kiss on the cheek. "You're so cute! Especially when you blush!" Elena beamed at him. "I'm glad we met, even if it was under stupid circumstances," Elena continued with a smile. Somehow, women who didn't waste any time made him a little suspicious. As irritated as he was by her forwardness, he enjoyed every touch. Jean secretly hoped she would kiss him again.

Elena sensed this instinctively. "Should I make us a pot of coffee?"

"Yes, please. With milk and sugar!" he replied, a little relieved.

"If you want, you can smoke a cigarette in the meantime. I'm going to freshen up. Please smoke on the porch. There's an ashtray outside."

Jean nodded, went outside, and smoked. He enjoyed every puff in the mild night air. He looked up at the sky, where the stars sparkled differently than usual.

"What a night," he thought. Despite his injuries, Jean felt nothing but euphoria.

When he had finished his Lucky, he was astonished to see Elena come out onto the balcony wearing only a negligee, with a large coffee cup in her hand. Jean wasn't quite sure how to react to her change of outfit. However, he felt his masculinity reacting immediately.

"Thank you, Elena. Look at the stars, great night, isn't it?" he said awkwardly. 'You didn't tell me you ride a motorcycle!' Jean pointed to the leather clothes hanging up.

Elena made a dismissive gesture with her right hand. Then she replied, "Yes, they're mine, but unfortunately I don't have my own motorcycle at the moment. I rode around the area a bit yesterday with a friend." That settled the matter, and Elena snuggled up to Jean, who was getting hotter and hotter in the mild night air.

Jean finally returned her caresses, lovingly stroking Elena's open hair. They kissed passionately. "Come on, let's go inside," she said finally. "There are too many onlookers here on the balcony. Besides, I haven't shown you the most comfortable room in my little apartment yet!"

When they reached the bedroom, she smiled ravishingly at him. Jean returned her gaze and sensually slipped the straps of her negligee off her shoulders. Elena's body shivered. The smooth, flowing fabric caressed her still firm breasts as it fell. Her cheeks flushed.

Then he knelt in front of her. He kissed her flat upper abdomen. At the same time, he caressed her waist and her beautiful, round bum with his strong hands. She moaned softly, took his face in both hands. Then she whispered, "Te quiero! I want you!" She tenderly pulled him up to her.

Full of anticipation, she kissed him. Elena caressed his neck with her hot lips. Her supple fingers skillfully exposed his manhood, which stretched lustfully toward her. His body trembled with excitement. "I want you!" was his only thought.

Driven by animal passion, they made love until Elena and Jean lay exhausted but satisfied in each other's arms. She enjoyed his love-drenched body while she wondered when she had last been loved like this. Jean felt the same way. She had completely enchanted him.

Only after she had dropped him off at his home did he realize that the accident had taken its toll. He must have suffered some bruises in the crash.

"It's not the end of the world," thought the expert. "The main thing is that I have her, or rather, she hit me ... And the damage to the Triumph motorcycle isn't that dramatic either."

He was violently torn from his romantic thoughts when he realized that the gate to his house had been broken open.

Then he heard his dog growling and ran to the front door, which was wide open. Only when he turned on the light did the appraiser see that his apartment was in complete chaos. The white-painted front door and hallway were covered in bloodstains. All the furniture had been knocked over, but he didn't care about that right now. He had only one thought. Was Arthos okay? Jean heard his Doberman growl again. He was startled when something pressed against his leg from behind. Sarre looked around frantically, then he saw him. Arthos sat down next to his master. The dog was covered in blood. However, Jean quickly realized that the blood wasn't his. It looked like he had bitten the burglar badly. The big dog first licked his hand tenderly but then barked at him reproachfully. He limped a little, but didn't seem to be injured otherwise. Exhausted, Arthos lay down in his usual place in front of the leather couch.

The Doberman had driven the intruder away, but now Sarre had to make sure that nothing was missing. Was his "booty" still in its hiding place? He breathed a sigh of relief when he realized that Arthos hadn't given the robber a chance to steal even a crumb of bread.

"Good boy, you've earned yourself a bone every day for that," Jean said quietly to his dog. But his Doberman was already asleep, snoring softly on his dog blanket. No wonder, because his day had been anything but quiet.

When his owner saw him lying there, he realized that he too was exhausted. Nevertheless, he opened a can of Spanish beer, which he only drank half of. Jean decided to sleep for at least three hours. Neither the blood-stained front door nor the overturned furniture interested him tonight. But tomorrow morning, he would take care of it first thing.

Jean sat down on his couch and fell asleep immediately. However, he couldn't find any peace. His sleep was punctuated by nasty nightmares.

He had only slept for two and a half hours when the doorbell rang several times. Amid loud barking, the expert opened the front door just a crack. He was careful not to touch the dried blood. "Ah, it's you! Good morning, Inspector. Please wait a moment, I have to let my dog out behind the house first." "Bon dia, Señor Sarre! Yes, please do. I was going to suggest that anyway. Your Doberman doesn't seem very friendly!" said Carlos Ruiz to Jean.

Sarre noticed that the policeman's voice was slightly shaky at times. "Arthos is a bit suspicious at the moment. He didn't have a great night either! But watch your clothes when you come in. You can see what it looks like in here!"

"Mierda, it looks really bad in here! Have you slaughtered a pig, Señor?" Jean calmly replied that an uninvited guest had made acquaintance with his dog. "Should I send for the forensic team? If you want, I'll call Roses right away," said Inspector Ruiz. 'No, don't bother, nothing's missing! Señor, you know how it is. Once the forensic team arrives with their brushes, it'll look worse than before. They won't find anything and will just leave graphite dust behind,' replied Jean Sarre. "Oh, by the way, Señor Sarre. The reason I stopped by... the Molotov cocktail... You were right, it was most likely not an accident. This morning, our French colleagues wanted to take a look at the apartment of photographer Gerard Brieaux in Perpignan, but someone beat them to it. It must have been quite a mess there. I feel sorry for our colleagues. After all, they have to write the report." "Well, yes," replied Jean with a grin. 'But you're in charge of the murder, so your report will probably be a bit longer.' The inspector didn't bat an eyelid, but Jean could tell he wasn't pleased with the remark. "Listen, Señor Sarre! If you think I'm lazy, that's your problem. But do you seriously believe this is the only thing I have to deal with?" Carlos Ruiz slowly worked himself into a rage. At the same time, Jean was annoyed by his sometimes cynical manner. "Oh, you know, Señor Sarre. You do your job and I'll do mine. I wonder why I'm here with you anyway, because I don't have to inform you about the status of the investigation!" The inspector headed for the door. Jean limped after him. His left leg had been more badly bruised in yesterday's accident than he wanted to admit. "Stay where you are... I'll find my way out on my own!" said Ruiz, looking him briefly but pointedly in the eye. Before Jean could smooth things over, the policeman had already closed the front door behind him.

Elena Lokova had once again come to the conclusion that you were best to do everything yourself. She hung up the phone angrily. The public phone booth must have suffered a lot since it was installed. The amateurish graffiti and chipped paint did not match the immaculate appearance of its user. Ms. Lokova was standing in downtown Figueres that morning. It was still very early, but she was already fed up. However, she could have guessed that these constantly stoned petty thieves were useless. The smell of coffee and fresh bread wafted temptingly from a street café that had just opened. Elena decided to have breakfast there. She hadn't really felt very hungry after the phone call, but last night had been quite short. She simply felt she needed to recharge her batteries before paying an unpleasant visit to two people.

Meanwhile, the trembling hand on the other end of the line slowly calmed down. The unkempt man ran his fingers frantically through his black, greasy hair. The Catalan stared apathetically out of the dilapidated three-room apartment at the still deserted streets of Figueres. He inhaled deeply on a hand-rolled cigarette before making his way to the bedroom. When he realized that the bedroom door was locked from the inside, he began to pound on it with both fists. Then the Spaniard began to shout angrily. "Fernando, you damn bum! Open the fucking door before I break it down!" It took almost a minute before there was any sign of movement on the other side of the door. For Pascal, it felt like an eternity. He was about to kick in the old wooden door when suddenly it slowly opened. An unshaven and sleepy face contorted into a tortured expression. "What the hell, Pascal, what the fuck is this? Leave the damn drugs alone in the morning!" Fernando was still standing in the doorway when his brother rushed at him. Pascal Cortez grabbed the younger Fernando by the collar. But he quickly let go when his brother began to whimper. "Aaah, ow! Damn it! You know that mutt, that damn fucking mutt, got me." Pascal took two steps back to look at his injured brother. For a moment, he even felt something like pity for him. Last night, Pascal had given the various bite wounds some temporary treatment, but now the bandages looked really bad. Coagulated blood mixed with soaked bandages.

If he couldn't get his brother to a hospital quickly, Fernando would at least have to deal with nasty infections. "We have a problem, Nando. But... I promise you, little brother... Everything will be fine!"

Dr. Eugenio Kremer heaved his heavy body into the leather executive chair, which creaked suspiciously. The doctor looked gloomy as he saw his plans slowly but surely slipping away. He still held all the cards, but he couldn't afford any more serious mistakes that would jeopardize his life's work. A few days ago, he had suggested to Señor Falgas that he bring his wife Mercedes to Vidasacra. At least here he would have her under control. But Juan Falgas simply couldn't bring himself to take that step. It was time for everything to change anyway. After all, he was doing all the work. So he no longer saw any reason to let his boss Falgas share in the profits to such an extent. Suddenly, there was a timid knock at the office door. The doctor was abruptly torn from his thoughts. When the door opened, a girl of about four entered with a mischievous smile.
"Hola! Uncle Eugenio, did you make my doll better?" The pretty blonde girl looked at Dr. Kremer expectantly with big, bright blue eyes. "Claro, my little Katharina!"
Smiling gently, the doctor reached under his desk. Shortly thereafter, he pulled out a small doll, whose broken leg he had glued back on last night between appointments.
"Look, sweetie! Your doll is all better. Now, Uncle Eugenio deserves a kiss, doesn't he?" Katharina quickly jumped toward Eugenio. The child gave him an exuberant kiss on

the cheek. "There you go, my little angel, now let Uncle Eugenio get back to work. I promise we'll go for a walk after dinner, Katharina. I also spoke to your mom on the phone. She's coming to visit us tomorrow. Maybe we should bake a nice cake for her? That would be a wonderful surprise! What do you think, Kathi?" Katharina was beside herself with excitement after the doctor mentioned her mother. Oh yes, Uncle Eugenio and she would bake a cake for her mom. That would be so great! Maybe her mother wouldn't have to leave right away? Kathi really liked the big house with all the rooms, but she would much rather be with her mom every day.

It was one of those gloomy, windy mornings. Juan Falgas got up quietly so as not to wake his wife Mercedes. Before leaving the large bedroom, the building contractor turned on his heel. He looked at his beautiful wife, who was pressing her jet-black hair into the soft pillows of the French bed. She sighed softly. It sounded almost like a cat purring. Juan had slept badly last night, but above all, he had had very bad dreams. Only he couldn't remember the details of his nightmare. Something about a forest clearing, a single tree ... monsters that wanted to devour him.
But he couldn't remember the context. He probably only had these dreams because he had received a call from Vidasacra the night before. That unpleasant Dr. Kremer actually wanted to invite him and his wife to dinner. What was this brazen guy up to? Juan gradually began to think

that he should get rid of this insolent doctor as quickly as possible.

The photographer was dead! Dead people don't talk, as we all know. It was incredibly difficult for him to say nothing when Mercedes put the newspaper aside with tears in her eyes.

Somehow, Juan had the vague feeling that everything had been slipping away from him lately. He had also been feeling a certain apathy for a while. It was probably comparable to a psychosomatic wall that he couldn't get through.

Oh yes, how he had desired this woman. Juan had been feeling very attracted to his wife again for a long time. So strongly that he felt a pleasant sensation in his groin. He quietly approached the large bed. Smiling, Falgas slowly pulled the thin quilt aside. Mercedes lay there as God had created her. The Spanish woman instinctively pulled her slender legs toward her as a cool breeze touched her flawless body. Still half asleep, a soft moan escaped her lips.

Meanwhile, Juan let his pajamas slide to the floor. He lay down carefully behind his beautiful wife. He tenderly began to kiss her back, all the way up to her slender neck. At the same time, he cupped her breast with his right hand. While Juan caressed her shapely breasts, he pressed himself harder and harder against his wife's sun-tanned body. On the verge of being overcome by his arousal, the building contractor felt as if he had been transported back in time. Now Mercedes let out a voluptuous, long moan and reached for the fingers that were massaging her breasts. When she guided his hand deep down between her wet thighs, Juanito began to sigh softly. How long had it been since they last slept together? Juan pressed himself harder and harder against Mercedes. Now he tried frantically to penetrate her. Finally, she opened herself to him. Full of lust, he began to savor it slowly. For a moment, he really felt like he could turn back time. But how could that work? His young wife Mercedes had been looking at him lately as if the devil himself were standing in front of her. Didn't she understand why he was working so hard? But such thoughts only flashed through his mind for a few milliseconds. What mattered was the "here and now!" At that moment, Falgas felt as if his balls were as big as coconuts. A strong desire drew him more and more into its spell. "Oh yes, my love," whispered Mercedes in a half-sleep, "Oh yes, Gerard, come, Gerard!"

Juan Falgas suddenly felt nothing but blind rage. All desire was gone. He grabbed his wife's slender neck from behind. As if he were out of his mind, he began to shake and choke her. The transition from love, passion, and hate suddenly seemed fluid.

Mercedes was suddenly wide awake. Panicked, she coughed and gasped for air. The young woman tried to speak, but her constricted throat would not allow it. Juan's wife tried to turn around. But she couldn't free herself from his tight grip. Then she felt his grip loosen. The next moment, she was knocked to the floor by a painful kick. Out of the corner of her eye, she saw her gasping husband. Somehow, she didn't really understand what had just happened. Slowly but surely, Mercedes tried to make sense of it all.

She must have been dreaming just a moment ago, but what had happened then? Her sometimes choleric husband often treated her badly, but he had never hit his wife before. Juan had raped her mentally many times, but physically? Then she heard him slam the bedroom door. Intimidated, Mercedes lay on the cool floor for quite a while.

Jean Sarre's emotional life had also been in turmoil for a long time. He was really taken with Elena. Somehow, he felt like he was on cloud nine. However, he also began to wonder what the extremely attractive woman saw in him. Maybe she just wanted a man? Had he read too much into it? After all, Jean didn't consider himself a ladies' man or someone who understood women. Besides, the connection didn't really come at a good time, because Jean suspected that his find would cause him problems. He needed a clear head. Such a distraction was rather counterproductive.

Sarre didn't believe that the break-in had anything to do with his unexpected windfall. After all, there were break-ins here all the time. Meanwhile, it was no longer just a matter of Spanish junkies committing crimes to support their habit. Since the fall of the Berlin Wall, several Eastern European gangs had also been up to no good in the area. He had recently read in the newspaper that the police had broken up a Romanian burglary gang.

Jean sat in front of the house on a step, drinking a cup of instant coffee and thinking. Every now and then he glanced down at his dog, who had once again made himself comfortable at his feet. Maybe Jean should deposit the money somewhere else? But he couldn't very well go to the bank to deposit half a million euros into his account. He might as well take the money straight to the cops. They would probably lock him up immediately.

His motorcycle was still standing in front of the garage, just as he had left it the night before. Armed with his tool bag, he set about removing the battered plastic parts. When he unscrewed the seat, he couldn't believe his eyes.

What was that? Something had been attached to the rear wheel cover with tape.

Suddenly, Jean Sarre's heart was in his mouth. He looked at the taped-on part and quickly realized what it was. It was a GPS tracking device. The little bug was already dirty, so he had been driving around with the mini transmitter for some time. Someone had most likely been following him. That someone knew he had something that didn't belong to them. Jean immediately set about searching his SUV for another transmitter. The expert quickly found what he was looking for under the rear bumper of the Land Cruiser.

Jean Sarre stood in front of the house with the two transmitters in his hands. Every now and then he saw cheerful tourists strolling past on the other side of the entrance gate. Suddenly there was a loud bang. Jean flinched involuntarily, and both bugs fell to the sandy ground in front of him.

CHAPTER 4: *Frost Angel and the hunting moon*

Elena Lokova put her chrome cell phone back in her black handbag. Shortly thereafter, she pushed open the heavy door. The light flickered sporadically in the hallway. There was a pungent smell of decay and urine. Garbage was piled up everywhere. Most of the residents of this social housing project could probably be described as completely neglected by society.

Elena reached a rooftop apartment on the fourth floor after climbing a stone staircase littered with mouse droppings.

There was no name on the doorbell, but that was not unusual in these apartment blocks.

She pressed the bell briefly, which emitted only a faint whimper. At the same time, she knocked on the small, scratched front door with her left hand. She noticed that someone inside was fiddling with the peephole. It would have been easy to blow this person's brains out at that moment. Her slender right hand instinctively touched the large-caliber pistol she was carrying in a shoulder holster hidden under her light summer jacket.

Slowly and creakingly, the door opened. A sweaty man looked up at her uncertainly.

"Thank goodness, Señora. Come in! My brother needs a doctor urgently! He's been bitten all over by that fucking mutt." Elena entered the small, run-down apartment with a reproachful sigh.

Then the Russian woman turned to Pascal without really looking at him.

"You and your brother are really the worst!" Elena hissed. The tall blonde had to control herself. "You can't have screwed everything up! You knew about that damn dog and all you had to do was use pepper spray to incapacitate it. You don't seriously believe you're going to be rewarded for this botched job."

Elena was boiling with rage, because to her, the two whiny Cortez brothers weren't even amateur burglars. She wouldn't spend a penny on them, let alone a bullet.

In the meantime, Fernando also emerged from the musty bedroom. Elena looked at him. For a brief moment, she even felt pity for Pascal's younger brother.

Fernando stared more or less apathetically into space. The poor guy couldn't utter a single word. His makeshift bandages were almost falling off.

Somehow, the young man reminded Elena of an ancient Egyptian mummy who, after thousands of years, was finally allowed to attack the living. Or perhaps more like a zombie who had just escaped from the morgue. "Pascal, can you see the angel too?" whispered Fernando. The injured man pointed at Elena with trembling hands. Feverish shivers ran through Fernando's body. But he slowly stumbled toward the tall blonde woman. Pascal grabbed him by the arm before he could reach her and manhandled him back into the bedroom. "Rest, brother, the angel will help you," he said and closed the door behind Fernando. "Can't you see what's going on? Look how bad my brother is. Take him to a doctor, or he'll die."

Elena had to promise that she would take care of Fernando. She would drive him to a doctor first thing in the morning. "Why wait until tomorrow? He might be dead by then!"

Pascal looked at Elena like a man dying of thirst in the desert begging for a glass of water.

Then the woman took a small bottle from her handbag and gave it to him.

"Here, give him three of these pills every two hours. Make sure he drinks plenty of water. I'll take him to the doctor tomorrow morning!" she said. Pascal took the medicine but didn't say another word. With a lump in his throat, he looked into the Russian woman's face. The petty criminal felt a chill run through him. He didn't like the look in her steel-blue eyes at all.

Without another word, Elena left the apartment and slammed the battered front door behind her. Once again, she was convinced that it was best to do everything herself.

Now she would have to put all her acting skills to use once again.

The old Harley-Davidson that roared past Jean Sarre's house was what gave him such a fright. Someone could have stabbed him with a needle at that moment. He certainly wouldn't have bled. The misfiring of the poorly tuned engine was the last straw for Jean's nerves that day, especially since he had found the two mini transmitters.

Sarre took the Glock 17 pistol out of its hiding place, just to be on the safe side. Then he inserted a magazine filled with 17 cartridges into the weapon. He sat on the leather couch with his dog at his feet, locked the front door, and stared at the black 9mm lying on the table in front of him. He had been familiar with weapons since his time in the military. The last few years had also forced him to deal with them from time to time. However, it had been quite a while since he had last fired a gun. So he wondered whether he should do some target practice again. It couldn't do any harm, at least. Besides, no one would be interested in a little shooting in the backwoods.

Jean got up and went to the fridge to take out a can of beer. Somehow, the ice-cold metal felt good against his sweaty hands. Sarre glanced at the can briefly. But then he put it back in the fridge with the others. Instead, he made himself an instant coffee. Jean sighed as he placed the steaming cup on the table in front of him. Arthos watched with interest at first, then yawned profusely. Somehow, his master had changed dramatically over the last few days. He could smell the adrenaline and sweat. It was a mixture of smells that the Doberman didn't really like. Jean's gaze wandered from his cigarette pack to the self-loading pistol. "Great still life! Both can kill!" he thought. The specialist noticed that it wasn't just his hands that were sweating. He stood up again, reached for the brandy bottle, and poured himself a generous shot into his coffee. Then Falgas took the black pistol in his right hand. With his left hand, he inserted a seventeen-round magazine into the weapon. He pulled back the slide. He let it snap forward again, "Rat-rat." He immediately relaxed again. Only to then aim at the white front door. Shortly thereafter, Jean removed the magazine, pulled the slide back again to remove the cartridge that was still in the chamber. Then he repeated the whole process. He took the pistol apart, put it back together ... He did this several more times to make sure he was confident. In the past, Jean could have dismantled, cleaned, and reassembled the pistol blindfolded and in the middle of a firefight. But that was a long time ago, and he lacked practice. He had never been a gun enthusiast. For him, guns were nothing more than tools used for hunting and fighting. Slowly but surely, he became calmer. Sarre resolved not to let himself be taken by surprise again. The expert had to reattach the transmitters to his vehicles so that they wouldn't know what was going on. They should believe that he was easy prey and that he had no idea what was going on. They wanted the money, but they could forget about him voluntarily handing over half a million dollars. Jean had to see behind the façade, had to know what this was all about. Then he could react before they did. He couldn't wait until they had him cornered. "First strike," he said aloud. "First strike," because attack was known to be the best form of defense. But inside, the cautious Sarre felt anything but brave and confident.

"Shit, mierda!" he thought. "Pull yourself together, are you still a man or have you turned into a mouse?" Jean noticed that his hands were starting to sweat again. He said reproachfully to himself, "More like a mouse!" Then he tucked the pistol into the back of his waistband. Side by side with his dog, he walked onto the porch. The two strolled peacefully past the swimming pool. There was a palm tree behind an old stone wall.

The solid wall separated the property from the neighbors. However, the expert had not yet seen his neighbor. After looking around briefly, Jean pulled a sandstone out of the wall and pushed it back in. His treasure was well hidden. For the moment, the half a million was safe here.

His observers were probably expecting him to find another hiding place. By breaking in, they wanted to make him so nervous that he would take the money somewhere else.

"That's it!" he thought, and his tense expression suddenly brightened. He would do them this favor.

The small lake below the winding road lay calm and peaceful in the evening sun. Tourists rarely strayed here because the path leading to it was difficult to access. Jean Sarre had discovered this picturesque spot not long ago. Above the lake was a conifer grove consisting mainly of pine and fir trees. Accessible only via a small footpath, about 550 yards further on stood the ruins of a farmhouse that had probably been abandoned several years ago. On weekends, a few locals always came to the lake to fish or have a barbecue with their families. The place had also long been a romantic secret spot for lovers. You could tell just by the number of discarded condoms. However, to drive right up to the lake shore, you had to use an off-road vehicle, because for a normal sedan, or rather its oil pan, the drive there could be described as rather unhealthy.

Jean Sarre also went fishing, but he didn't need a fishing rod for his plans, just a tin box. After the old four-wheel drive Toyo had bravely overcome the torturous route, Arthos and his master got out right at the lake shore. To make sure they were really alone there at the moment, they both went for a walk first. Then Jean put his dog back in the car. Then Sarre took a worn backpack and strapped it awkwardly onto his back. The evening sun was still shining brightly, and he would be able to do some shooting practice in this idyllic setting, he told himself as he walked up the sandy footpath to the dilapidated farmhouse. He looked around from time to time. He had deliberately parked his car so that he could see it at all times. He had to hurry. The sun would set in half an hour at the latest.

When he reached the ruins, he took off his backpack. Then he took out the pistol and a full magazine. Three empty wine bottles lay nearby in the undergrowth, and Jean placed them on a small ledge where two lizards were basking in the evening sun.

One of them glanced at Jean in alarm, then the small, pale yellow reptiles disappeared like lightning between the old broken stones. Sarre moved about twenty meters away from his temporary targets. He had a good view from this position. His SUV was still standing alone on the shore of the lake. It didn't look like he had any unwelcome company either. Jean loaded the Glock. Next, he aimed at the left of the three bottles. In these lighting conditions, it was impossible to distinguish between white and green glass, but that wasn't really necessary. Jean's hand trembled slightly, so he lowered the pistol again. "It's all in the breathing," he thought, and aimed again as he exhaled. Then he pulled the trigger. The shot went off—and missed. "Well, I'm a little out of practice, but practice makes perfect, as they say!" The second shot shattered the bottle into a thousand pieces, but only after he had reduced the distance to a "rookie-friendly" fifteen meters. At this shorter range, the remaining two bottles were also quickly dealt with. Jean was well aware, however, that he would not be competing in any handgun competitions anytime soon. But then again, he didn't necessarily want to be a sharpshooter. With a ringing in his ears, Jean returned to his backpack. He took out a folding spade and the metal box. So, where was the best place to bury it? He looked around and found a spot that seemed ideal for his purpose. After digging about five feet deep, Sarre wiped the sweat from his forehead. Then he placed the empty metal box in the hole. He quickly shoveled it back in, shouldered his backpack, and hurried back the way he came. Down by his car, Jean wondered how quickly he could get back there.

The sun had almost set. The full moon was now peeking through the clouds. Jean looked around once more. After glancing at his watch, he sped off toward Empuriabrava in his Land Cruiser.

There was quite a lot of traffic on the roads. The tourists all seemed to be heading out for dinner at the same time. Sarre tried to stay cool, but nevertheless overtook a few cars.

He turned off his car radio so as not to be distracted from his thoughts. All kinds of memories from his former life rained down on him. If what he feared happened, he would have to revive the "former" Jean.

He was actually a little afraid of that. But it was his own fault. If he had just done his job, he probably wouldn't be in this dangerous situation now. His curiosity alone, but perhaps also his greed, had brought him here.

When he arrived home, the appraiser felt both excited and exhausted. But he couldn't waste any time. Sarre immediately drove the car into the garage. He removed the mini transmitter and carefully placed it on the garage floor. Jean quickly drove the Toyota out again. Even as a little boy, he had often gone hunting with his grandfather. He remembered this vividly on the drive back to the small lake. More than once, the two of them had sat silently in the forest, waiting for prey near the "bait site" or the "Kirrung". Jean's grandfather was a hunter with heart and soul. His grandson had inherited some of this passion for hunting.

The first thing to do now was to hide the Toyota. The expert knew where. About a kilometer from the lake, the sandy dirt roads forked. If he took the right one, he would drive straight into the woods. There was a small depression near a dry creek bed.

When he got out and turned off the headlights, the full moon appeared in all its glory. It was almost too bright. Well, at least he didn't need any artificial light to find his way around.

"Hunting moon," thought the expert. Now he felt his tiredness disappear. "Except that we're not going boar hunting, or are we?" The thought made him grin involuntarily. Jean let Arthos jump out. However, he told him not to bark. Then he grabbed his pistol. Both crept in the shadows of the old pine trees toward the ruins of what had once been a farm. On the way through the woods, Jean felt more alive than he had in a long time. The full moon was shining so brightly that he didn't even need his flashlight. It smelled like rosemary. Every now and then, an owl hooted. But even though the crickets were still chirping loudly, Jean heard the sound of a car not far away.

After another twenty yards, Arthos and his owner were very close to the farm ruins. Now the only question was whether the occupants of the car were love-struck teenagers or his surveillance team. Sarre hoped for the latter. If his trap snapped shut, he could clear up all the questions tonight.

Arthos growled briefly, but Jean signaled him to lie down and keep quiet. In the moonlight, he saw an old Land Rover arrive. When a figure got out and ran around searching, Jean's heart beat faster. Now the person went back to the car and returned with a shovel. No doubt about it, Jean's plan had worked.

When the figure began digging for Jean's metal box, the appraiser slowly crept up from behind.

"You there, hands up and turn around!"

Jean's voice trembled like a leaf. He also felt as if his legs were suddenly made of jelly. The stranger threw the shovel aside and turned abruptly, but without raising his arms. A chrome pistol glinted in the moonlight. Jean wanted to shoot, but he had completely forgotten to load the gun. So all that could be heard was a click. Something like this would never have happened to him before. At that moment, Arthos rushed past Jean from behind. The Doberman wanted to pounce on the stranger. Then a single shot rang out. Arthos yelped briefly and fell to the ground bleeding. Jean pulled back the slide of the Glock and fired several shots at the stranger in a rage. "Damn you, you dirty, damn pig!" Jean was beside himself with rage. The dark figure dropped his weapon. He spun around once more, then fell onto his stomach with a groan. Jean quickly grabbed the shiny silver weapon. Not without first staring hatefully at the now lifeless body. He ran back to Arthos, who was lying on the sandy ground, whimpering. Jean had to stop the bleeding, so he tore his T-shirt to bandage the gunshot wound. When he had finished giving his loyal friend first aid, he took the flashlight to shine it on the stranger. When he shone the light on his opponent's face, Jean Sarre felt like he was about to lose his mind.

At around the same time, Dr. Eugenio Kremer sat in his hospital cafeteria armed with a large piece of cream cake. Here in Vidasacra, the world was still in order. However, he had to keep both his staff and his "organ donors" under control. By now, his employees knew what would happen to them if they said a word to anyone outside the hospital.
Dr. Eugenio Kremer was always up to date in his job.

Organ trafficking was booming. In Europe alone, around 40,000 people were currently waiting for a kidney donor. Around 5,000 people in Spain were still hoping for an organ donation.

Kidney patients topped the waiting list with an estimated 4,500, followed by liver patients with 1,000. Around 150 people were waiting for a lung donation, a new heart would save the lives of 100 patients, 90 Spaniards needed a new pancreas, and around 10 people with intestinal diseases were waiting for a new digestive system. The kidney trade was particularly flourishing. After all, the kidney is the only organ that can be removed without killing the patient. But the black market also offered livers, eyes, heart valves, parts of the brain—practically everything.

This was exactly where the money was to be made, and so Kremer created a thriving transplant tourism industry. Over the last few years, the Pedro Leon Clinic had been converted into a high-security wing. In addition, Dr. Kremer and Juan Falgas had built a stately villa with the telling name "Salvation" near the hospital. Here, the newly operated customers were to be able to recover in extreme comfort and peace.

As Dr. Kremer was absentmindedly devouring the cream cake, his head nurse approached him from behind. "Hola, Doc, how's my homemade cake?"

"Claro, my dear Rita. It's delicious, as always! What's new with our donors? Have you done the blood tests?" Head nurse Rita leaned her hands on the table. Then she bent forward so that Dr. Kremer had a good view of her cleavage.

"Sure, Doc, the test results are on your desk," she purred, "but some of the new arrivals from last week are sick, you already know that!"

"Well, my dear, then do everything you can to separate the sick from the healthy. Then carry out more blood tests!"

Head nurse Rita nodded. She wondered secretly whether she would be able to please the good doctor tonight. Not that she particularly enjoyed it. But the fat little doctor never took long and was usually grateful afterwards. Besides, he had given her a raise last month. She had promptly ordered a new car. Rita was also one of the few people on the team who knew pretty much what was going on. That's why she had permission to travel and use her own cell phone. Rita was a few years older than Eugenio, and the two met in Madrid. At the time, they were working in the same hospital. Eugenio was a newly qualified doctor, and the well-proportioned woman was a nurse. Rita almost got into trouble with the narcotics law back then, but Dr. Eugenio Kremer covered it up. Since then, she had been deeply grateful to him, and over time, this gratitude had even developed into a kind of servitude. Despite this emotional dependence, the two rarely addressed each other informally. Perhaps after a successful cunnilingus or fellatio. At this thought, Rita smiled as her tongue unconsciously ran over her upper lip.

"Rita, listen! Tomorrow morning, a rich guy from Austria is landing at Girona airport. I assume Jaques will fly him here in his helicopter." The doctor took off his glasses and smiled at his head nurse with his small eyes.

"Claro! Of course I know that. Everything will be done to your satisfaction, Jefe!" Rita replied with a smile.

"Good, I already know which kidney we're going to remove. According to my records, it's one from No. 943. Is that okay?" said the doctor, continuing to talk to his head nurse.

Then Rita replied intently:

"The blood type is a match! Kidney disease can be ruled out in No. 943.

The tests were positive ... Medical history, physical examination with blood pressure measurement, blood values, kidney values, electrolytes, urine values, protein, cells, microscopy, and ultrasound.

Then there's the tissue typing ... Of course, as always, we'll check whether the operation can be performed without any major medical risks and how the blood supply to the kidneys is."

"No problem, as long as the Colombian doesn't get sick," replied Kremer. They agreed that the Colombian 'donor' would then 'discharge'. Perhaps one or two organs could be sold to business associates if necessary.

"Patient 943 still has a wife and two children," Rita whispered quietly to Dr. Kremer. The doctor scratched his ear and whispered back. "Tell his family that their father has been released from quarantine. They can see him soon. I also received an email three days ago. Someone urgently needs a child's heart."

"That's what I call coincidence," said head nurse Rita, turning around and swaying her hips as she left the canteen. "Doctor, if you need me, you know …"
Dr. Kremer grinned and watched his head nurse walk away. "I know, I know. Everything's under control!"

Elena Lokova tried to reach Jean on his cell phone for the fifth time, but without success. She was sure he was at home. After all, that's what her tracking device was showing. Well, maybe he was out walking the dog. At that moment, Elena hoped that her business partners wouldn't go ahead without her. She would "smooth things over"; after all, she was an expert, and not just since yesterday. On the other hand, her professionalism was beginning to crumble slightly when it came to Jean Sarre. Last night had been fantastic. Although sex was just a means to an end, she couldn't think about anything else. She was now in her late forties, but she had never experienced anything like this before. Jean was the first man who had shown her that love play could be different.
An orgasm, multiple orgasms! For Elena, the myth had become reality last night. It had been over twenty hours now, but Elena still felt him between her thighs.
"Sweet sweat!" she thought, but at the same time, the Russian woman tried to banish these lustful shivers from her mind.

At the same time, Jean was also struggling with sweat. However, it was more a mixture of sweat from exertion and fear. Paralyzed, he had dragged the dead body by its legs into the ruins. Then he carried his whimpering dog through the darkness to the car. At least the full moon briefly illuminated the area and showed Jean the way.

Wrapped in a blanket, he immediately drove his dog to a nearby veterinary clinic. As he got out of the car in front of the building, a younger veterinarian he knew by sight was just leaving. The vet awkwardly locked the glass entrance door.

"Hola y Buenas Noches, Doctor. Come on! You have to help us!" Jean called to the young veterinarian. The latter looked a little puzzled, but then came toward Jean, more or less indignant.

"Drive on... to Figueres, to the clinic! I'm off duty now," the veterinarian replied gruffly.

"You're going to take care of my dog, do you understand!" Jean had to pull himself together to keep from yelling. The veterinarian was planning to simply ignore him. Jean suddenly felt like a little schoolboy who wasn't being taken seriously. He stood in the man's way and drew his gun. He didn't care about anything anymore; after all, he had just killed a person.

"We're going to your clinic together! You're going to treat my dog, understand? Besides, it won't be your loss ... if he survives! If you just let him die, I'll shoot you. You wouldn't be the first!"

"Do you understand?" The young veterinarian understood. Beads of sweat formed on his high forehead and he opened the glass door again, trembling.

Arthos had been really lucky. A clean shot through and through. Thank God that damn bastard had used full metal jacket bullets. With deformation or even expansion bullets, the Doberman would most likely not have had a chance. During the operation, the men had talked quietly. The young veterinarian told Jean a few things about his life. Jean now knew that Dr. Pedro Vasquez was struggling with serious financial problems. His wife suffered from multiple sclerosis and their child had recently been hit by a car. Pedro worked a lot. However, the money he earned as a veterinarian was not nearly enough to make ends meet.

"Listen, Doctor Vasquez! Let's make a deal!
You forget the last two hours, and I'll bring you twenty thousand euros! Deal, hombre?"

Pedro Vasquez nodded with a smile and hesitantly agreed. He should have called the police because of the gunshot wound. Not to mention that the stranger had threatened him with a gun.

But what would he gain from that? He could really use the promised twenty thousand euros.

Doctor Vasquez solemnly explained to Jean that the Doberman was now out of danger. In all likelihood, he would pull through. However, the dog would need a few more hours of rest.

Jean pondered. The veterinarian suggested that he leave the dog there. "I'll take good care of him when the anesthesia wears off, señor! Come back tomorrow around noon and please ... bring the money with you." After he left the office, his thoughts began to spin. It was still night, but the sun would rise in about an hour.

First, Sarre had to return to the old ruin. Should he put the body in the Land Rover and then sink it in the lake? No, that wouldn't work! Jean was still driving around in the Land Cruiser with the Stihl chainsaw. He had to get rid of the body somehow. Just the thought of having to dismember it made Jean feel nauseous.

When Sarre returned to the dilapidated farmhouse, he couldn't believe his eyes. The Land Rover was gone. Had he just dreamed it all? He jumped out of the car and ran to where he had left the body hours earlier. But it was gone too.

The small, dead, unfriendly policeman named "Quitano" was nowhere to be found. Jean Sarre stood in front of the ruins in disbelief. He looked around frantically in all directions.

"Damn it, since when can dead people walk? That idiot can't have turned into a zombie!"

The expert tried to find footprints. He found at least some drag marks. Someone must have dragged his dead adversary out of the ruins and taken him away in the old Landy. But who, for God's sake, would want to do his dirty work? What reason could there be for doing so? And why was this cop involved?

Quitano must have been secretly watching him lately.

Jean was also certain that Arthos had saved his life. If the Doberman hadn't caught the bullet from the silver Sig Sauer pistol, he would now be lying somewhere with a 9mm projectile in his chest.

It was self-defense, wasn't it? Jean tried to review the situation.

However, even the most diverse perspectives did not change the fact that Jean had killed a Spanish police officer. That was definitely life imprisonment.

A few hours later, after he had returned home, his phone rang. Jean answered, and a visibly calmer female voice greeted him on the other end.

"Hola Jean, I thought you had emigrated! I called you several times last night, but you didn't answer."

Elena's melodious voice was now like balm for his battered soul.

"I'm sorry," he replied hesitantly. "But I haven't been feeling very well since yesterday."

"You poor darling, unfortunately I have to go out this morning. But I promise I'll take care of you as soon as I get back!"

Elena continued to sweet-talk him for a while, but after Jean agreed euphorically, she hung up.

The expert was just about to recover from the exertions of the previous night when someone rang the doorbell.

Sarre had a bad feeling about this. When he opened the door a crack, he looked into the tired face of Detective Inspector Ruiz.

CHAPTER 5: *The bad decision*

Elena Lokova skillfully navigated her black Golf GTI through the morning traffic in Figueres. Next to her in the passenger seat sat an extremely nervous small-time crook named Pascal.

Meanwhile, his brother Fernando lay feverishly moaning in the back seat of the Volkswagen. "Damn it, tell your brother to shut up!" Elena snapped at her passenger. "Señora, you have to understand ... Nando is dying. He has a high fever. Where are you taking us?" Pascal was already at the end of his tether. But the blonde Señora and the prospect of seeing a doctor were his only hope at the moment.

Elena replied hesitantly. "Where do you think? To a hospital ... as promised!"

From Figueres, they drove via Besalú and Ripoll towards Andorra. They drove for hours on bumpy roads in the Pyrenees. Although the landscape was very beautiful, none of the passengers had any appreciation for it.

The drive to Vidasacra took hours, and Elena turned on the car radio. She did this for several reasons. First, she wanted to be alone with her thoughts. She also couldn't stand Fernando's constant moaning anymore. Besides, she didn't feel like talking to Pascal.

On the one hand, Elena was overjoyed to see her daughter again. On the other hand, however, she knew that the visit to Vidasacra did not bode well.

When they arrived in the village, it was already noon. The Russian woman drove past the town sign. Then she turned into a small street that led past the cemetery. A large funeral procession was just passing along the narrow road. They had to wait a few minutes until the last of the mourners had crossed the path.

A little further on, they could see the large hospital building ahead of them. A helicopter flew thunderously overhead, landing on the tower of the green-painted hospital.

"What kind of strange hospital is this?" Pascal remarked when Elena had to briefly show her ID at a barrier. Several security guards were standing there talking. Now a huge man with a pockmarked face and a jet-black moustache emerged from his small gatehouse. When he recognized Elena, a brief smile crossed his lips.

But just as quickly as it had appeared, it disappeared again. It was probably just part of his job to look unfriendly. The man with the dangerous, downward-curving mustache and dark blue fantasy uniform slowly walked around the Golf and looked sternly into the car. Pascal glared back just as angrily. Almost at the same time, he spotted a rifle when his gaze wandered back to the gatehouse.

Leaning against the wall was a pump-action shotgun, a so-called "pump gun." "Hasta la vista, baby!" thought Pascal. What on earth was a goddamn hospital gatekeeper doing with a shotgun?

Did the pockmarked "Terminator" and his colleagues want to defend their hospital from strangers, or were patients who wanted to leave the hospital prematurely at their own risk ultimately shot at the gate? Pascal couldn't help but grin at the thought.

After the gate finally opened for Elena, Pascal, and Fernando, they came to a stop a few meters further on, in front of the main entrance. Only seconds later, two nurses ran toward them with a stretcher. The two men quickly loaded the moaning Fernando onto it. The nurses were clearly doing their best to handle the injured man as carefully as possible. His brother thanked them both.

Shortly after, a nurse dressed in white approached them and turned to Pascal with a smile.

"Hola, Señora y Señores, my name is Head Nurse Rita. Please follow me! I will take you to our visitors' room."

"Listen, nurse! My name is Pascal Cortez, please let me stay with my brother," replied the small-time crook. But Head Nurse Rita would not be moved.

"Señor Pascal, that's not possible, as we are about to take your brother into the operating room. You cannot be present during the treatment, of course! You understand, don't you?"

Pascal shrugged his shoulders, looked Rita deep in the eyes, then at her cleavage, before finally giving in. The sand-colored waiting room made a friendly impression. Nevertheless, Cortez couldn't help thinking that something was wrong with this hospital.

He sat down on a chair, stood up again, went to the sink in the corner, took a sip of water from the tap, then sat down again. Outside, two nurses were pushing his brother Fernando past on a mobile stretcher. Pascal could see them through a large glass pane.

"I have to get to him! He needs me! No matter what they say!" he thought. Pascal got up, left the room, and slowly followed them.

One of the two nurses awkwardly opened a glass door. Then they both wheeled Fernando, who was moaning softly, down a long, brightly lit corridor.

But even though all the operating rooms were on the left, they pushed the seriously injured man straight ahead to a freight elevator.

"The boss wants us to take him down to the basement. I don't understand. Can you make sense of it?" 'Listen, Carlito, do yourself a favor and don't worry too much,' replied the older of the two men in white quietly.

As they rode down in the elevator, Pascal noticed that a narrow staircase also led there. "Damn it, where are they taking Nando?" Pascal suddenly had an extremely queasy feeling in his stomach. As he crept after them down the stairs, his heart began to pound wildly.

When he reached the bottom, he peeked around the corner and just caught a glimpse of the two nurses, this time without Fernando, pushing their way back into the elevator. Since most of the ceiling lights were about to give out and were flickering wildly, the whole scene seemed somehow unreal.

It was also cold and quiet down here. Pascal could only hear soft voices coming from a room at the end of the hallway.

"Let's finish up here quickly, then we can take your little Katharina for a walk, if you like," said Dr. Kremer. Pascal then heard his employer reply.

"Eugenio, what are you up to? Why are we talking here in the basement? Why on earth aren't you taking care of the injured man? You should be in the operating room. After all, you told me on the phone to bring him to you so you could take care of him."

Elena's voice grew louder, but Eugenio just looked at her impishly from the side.

"But my dear, I'm taking care of the poor boy. See for yourself! I'm even going to give him some free heat treatment... hahahaha!"

When Eugenio saw Elena's utterly surprised face, he just laughed even louder.

Then the doctor simply pushed the stretcher to the other side of the room, to a small steel door. He quickly placed the quietly moaning Fernando in front of it.

"There you go, my boy. You'll feel better in no time!" Eugenio's voice was cold, mocking, and derisive. Even Elena felt a shiver run down her spine.

The doctor grabbed a pair of fireproof gloves and deftly unlocked the steel door. Now Dr. Eugenio Kremer simply lifted the stretcher into an inclined position. He patted Fernando's head almost tenderly once more, then slowly slid him into the oven, feet first.

Fernando Cortez was extremely weak in his feverish delirium, but when he realized what the crazy doctor was planning to do to him, he began to whimper violently. Seconds later, the seriously injured man was screaming in agony. However, it did him little good. The fire and heat crept slowly but inexorably up his legs. When the oven door finally closed behind the burning Fernando, it was all over.

Elena was speechless. Oh yes, she had certainly killed a few people, but the contract killer would never have done such a thing to one of her targets. It had usually been quick and painless.

"You're a fucking sadist!" The words came slowly and quietly from her lips. Eugenio was in the process of taking off his gloves, smiling at her, sweaty but triumphant.

When the doctor noticed that the Russian woman was staring at his crotch in irritation and disgust, he looked down at himself. He realized he had an erection. He awkwardly tried to hide it with his lab coat.

"There, my little killer," he tried to distract her. "See, I'm doing your work for you! Now kill his brother before I have to do it myself. You don't want to lose your job, do you?"

Elena looked at him with disgust. "And besides ..." Eugenio grinned and looked down at himself again. Then he took a small walkie-talkie out of his lab coat. "Nurse, please come to the basement room 'Numero Cinco' as soon as possible! I have a very satisfying task for you!"

There was a brief crackle, then the head nurse answered. Although the sound quality left much to be desired, the doctor learned that Rita was already on her way to them.

Pascal had only heard half of it from outside the door. But that was enough for him. The doctor, that fat pig, had simply killed his younger brother.

He wanted to storm into the room, but Pascal stood there, rooted to the spot. Now the lights went out. When the door opened, the Catalan had the presence of mind to hide behind a trolley.

Elena stepped out and went to the elevator to go upstairs. Now everything had to happen damn fast. That damn doctor should suffer just like Fernando. Pascal took a white coat from the clothes rack and slipped it on.

He slowly opened the door and entered the dark room. About three meters in front of him, Pascal heard a lustful moan.

"Good, good, good, Rita ... You're already here ... and I'm coming right now, haha mmmmh, yeahhh."

The next thing Eugenio Kremer felt was a hard kick in the middle of his extremely aroused genital area. The doctor simply buckled like a tree struck by lightning. He lay on the concrete floor with his pants down, gasping for air. Then the lights came back on. Pascal stood over him, filled with hatred, and spat into Eugenio's pain-contorted face.

"Well, you bastard, that feels good, doesn't it? Now I'm going to kill you, very slowly, just like you killed my brother!"

"Listen!" whimpered Kremer as he tried to pull up his pants.

"You misunderstand the situation! The woman, you see ... she forced me! If you want money, I'll give it to you ... I'll give you everything you want!"

Now Eugenio was crying openly.

Pascal spat at his feet in disgust.

"Señor, I beg you. I was forced! Please understand! Besides, your brother was already dead!"

Kremer tried everything to defuse the situation, but all his de-escalation strategies were in vain.

"You lying pig, fuck your damn money!" Pascal was beside himself with rage and punched the doctor's red face with full force. Eugenio Kremer's horn-rimmed glasses flew off his broken nose. Immediately afterwards, he spat blood. Pascal then manhandled the surgeon with a series of kicks towards the oven.

"Come on, open the oven door!" Pascal shouted, grabbing Eugenio by the collar. The doctor slowly got back to his feet. But instead of burning his fingers on the hot door, Eugenio suddenly spun around and lunged at Pascal.

Dr. Kremer held on to Pascal's coat with his left hand. Suddenly, a scalpel glinted in his right hand, which he used to stab his tormentor.

"Aaaah, you damn ..." Pascal broke free and tried to jump back. Kremer had hit him twice. His right thigh burned like hell and warm blood was already running over his shoes. Near the oven, there was a fire extinguisher attached to the wall. Pascal ripped it out of the wall along with its holder. Like a madman, he beat his opponent with it, who lay in front of him like a heap of misery on the concrete floor, not even twitching anymore.

Suddenly, Pascal saw his employer standing in the doorway with the head nurse. In slow motion, he realized that Elena was pointing a gun at him. He quickly threw the heavy fire extinguisher at her. Elena was hit with full force in the chest, fell dazedly against the door frame, and pulled Rita to the floor with her. Her gun slid across the room.

Pascal limped as fast as he could past the two women. He had to get out of there. He didn't even notice the black pistol lying on the floor about eight feet in front of him. He was convinced that he had avenged his brother. He was firmly convinced that he had beaten the mad doctor to death. Out in the hallway, he remembered that he couldn't just walk to the main entrance. The strange security guard would surely have been informed by now. Cortez had no desire to be shot. As if in a trance, he opened door after door. There had to be an emergency exit somewhere in the basement.

Suddenly, Pascal heard a voice he recognized. The two male nurses who had also led his brother to damnation were in a room that strongly resembled an operating theater.

"Okay, No. 943, you'll be discharged in a minute ... Hahaha," whispered one, squeezing hard. "Leave him alone, Carlito, what have you got against the man? He'll be dead soon anyway!"

The gagged Colombian lay on a wheeled stretcher, his arms and legs tied down with straps, forced to endure everything.

Somehow, Alberto Ziapata had imagined his future differently. The certainty that his wife Elvira and their two daughters Emilia and Johanna would most likely follow him to an early, violent death was bringing him to the edge of madness.

The whole ordeal for the Ziapata family began about seven months ago in a small, insignificant part of Colombia.

As is so often the case, or rather almost always, the prospect of a better life played a key role. Forty-five-year-old Alberto, an unskilled worker, had unexpectedly lost his job at a large agricultural company. From one day to the next, he had no idea how he was going to feed his family.

A few days after he was laid off, a casual acquaintance approached him out of the blue. Would he consider emigrating to Spain? A friend of his had connections to a large construction company in northern Spain. It would be a piece of cake to arrange something. The whole family would have to be shipped to Europe more or less illegally, but that wouldn't be a problem. As long as you could bribe one or two decision-makers.

Furthermore, that and the issuance of forged Spanish documents would be anything but inexpensive. But you would work something out, because Alberto could always put up his little house as payment. Alberto was certainly of two minds about the proposal. The Colombian asked for a few days to think it over. But the easily influenced man saw no future for himself and his family. So three days later, he agreed. In a small, dirty village pub, the deal that would change the Ziapata family's life forever was finally sealed.

Sitting next to Alberto were his acquaintance and a well-dressed agent. The agent praised Alberto's decision to the skies. He told Alberto that the Colombian would rise from a lowly laborer to a construction foreman in Spain in no time. In addition, after a proper education, his two daughters would certainly be able to study at a good, if not elite, university. Even his Elvira would have a better life in wealthy Europe, he was told.

Overwhelmed by the pompous phrases of the agent, who seemed extremely serious to Alberto, the Colombian agreed euphorically. After three large glasses of tequila, he finally signed over the family home. The small but charming house belonging to the Ziapata family was Elvira's pride and joy. Although Alberto's wife was even more simple-minded than her husband, Elvira at least felt that she had found happiness. She had married a hard-working, loyal man and given birth to two healthy daughters. After all, that was the most important thing.

What's more, her modest home gave her the opportunity to redecorate all the time.

Unfortunately, she recently lost her part-time job as a sales assistant, but Elvira always managed to make the best of the little that the family, or rather Alberto, earned.

Her two daughters also brought her great joy. Emilia and Johanna had grown into two well-behaved, pretty young ladies who helped their mother with the housework as best they could. Oh yes, Elvira was happy and content. At least until the day her husband told her they had to leave their home.

Lying on a stretcher, bound hand and foot, gagged and mocked, the poor Colombian was now aware of all his mistakes and weaknesses. If only he had stayed in his homeland with his family. Why did he have to let himself be talked into everything?

But he was just like the others who were locked up here. The prospect of a better life was a mirage. His brother had tried to dissuade him from traveling to Europe with his wife and two girls. But it was easy for him to say.

Alberto's brother still earned his living in Colombia. However, Alberto would rather have cut off his hand than take over his brother's job. He would never in his life have worked for the local drug cartel.

Although he could barely turn his head, Alberto suddenly noticed a fourth person in the small operating room. Pascal struck with an iron bar, moving so fast it was a blur.

The two male nurses didn't stand a chance of dodging the hard blows.

Pascal alternately beat the men in white coats until both of them lay motionless on the hard, blood-stained linoleum floor.

Then, completely out of breath, Pascal loosened the restraints and helped Alberto slowly sit up.

After being freed from his gag, Alberto rubbed his face frantically and stared at his rescuer in disbelief.

"Come on, man, let's go! We have to get out of here!" whispered Pascal.

"Mi Familia... my family... I have to get to them! My wife and my two daughters are still here!" Pascal pushed Alberto in front of him, completely annoyed. He would have liked to drive him forward with the heavy iron bar he was still holding in his hands, because he suspected they were close behind.

Slowly, the sedatives administered to Alberto began to take effect. "Hospital del Diablo... Hospital del Diablo... mi Familia..." he hissed repeatedly.

Pascal now had to support the visibly shaken Colombian.

Then suddenly they were outside. They had made it behind the hospital through an emergency exit.

About twenty meters in front of them, in a small parking lot, stood an ambulance with the driver's door open.

"Madre de Dios, we're damn lucky! Come on, hurry up!"

Pascal left his companion standing there for a moment and ran toward a Fiat Ducato that had been converted into an ambulance. At that moment, a shot rang out. Alberto screamed hoarsely and clutched his right arm.

"Damn it, what are you doing, where are you aiming? Shoot No. 943 in the legs! Don't shoot him in the stomach, come on!"

Pascal heard the words behind him and limped as fast as he could with his wounded leg, without turning around again.

The devil, it had to be the devil himself.

He could have sworn he had beaten the fat doctor, his brother's murderer, to death. How was such a thing possible?

He dove awkwardly into the driver's seat and screamed in pain. The key was in the ignition. He started the van and simply stepped on the gas.

Several shots rang out behind him. Pascal turned the car around and shifted into high gear. He sped off in the direction where he thought the exit slip was. But in all the excitement, he had lost his bearings. Then suddenly he saw the security guard.

In his imagination, he was standing right in front of him in his uniform, firing his 12/76 caliber shotgun.

The first shot blew the hood of the ambulance off and sent it flying through the air. The second shot smashed the windshield, but Pascal didn't let the third one hit. The Catalan slowed down briefly while kicking the windshield with all his might from the inside. Then he stepped on the gas again and hit the guard with full force. As Pascal ran him over, the ambulance jumped, or rather bounced, as if it were about to tip over at any moment.

"Must have had a shitty day!" Pascal allowed himself a slight grin and a quick glance in the rearview mirror.

There lay a lifeless man in a torn military-style uniform on the street, but behind him, he could see a person pointing a handgun at him.

There was a loud bang, then the ambulance spun like a top. The shooter had shot through a rear tire. Pascal had no chance of steering the vehicle in any direction and just held on to the steering wheel as tightly as he could.

"Mierda, fucking shit! Fernando, my brother, we'll see each other soon! If they don't want us in heaven, then we'll just party in hell!"

The car shot through a hedge, smashed through a fence, and rolled down a slope. Its driver didn't even notice that he had been thrown out and landed next to the car in the river. The strong current and icy water of the mountain river took Pascal's mind off his pain. The rushing water reminded him of angels carrying him away on light wings.

CHAPTER 6: *The Blackmail and the video*

"Buenos Dias, Señor Sarre. I need to talk to you urgently!" Inspector Ruiz stood in the doorway and looked tiredly at Jean. 'Hola Inspector, I was actually just about to lie down ... I hardly slept last night, please come back later,' replied Jean. But the policeman had already walked past him. He let himself fall onto Jean's leather couch with a swing.
"Forget it, Señor Sarre. We're going to talk about last night! Right now!"
Jean sensed that the game was over and his face turned red.
"You have two options, Señor!" The inspector stretched out comfortably on the couch. The expert stood in front of him like a schoolboy.
"Option A: You go to the slammer for murder, or option B: You do exactly what I tell you!"
"What do you want?" Jean replied meekly.
"Damn it, Sarre, who do you think got rid of Quitano's body? Think about it!"

Jean's brain cells tried to figure out how long a cop killer could survive in a Spanish prison. He probably wouldn't even make it through pretrial detention.

"Well ... my dear Jean," Carlos Ruiz suddenly said in a soft voice. "Quitano, that false dog, was watching you, and I was watching him, you understand?"

Jean didn't understand a thing. He shook his head briefly.

"Well, let's start from the beginning! Quitano was recently recommended to us by someone high up and presented a lot of good references. Strangely enough, however, he had no idea about police work, you understand?"

Jean remained silent.

"Two days after Gerard Brieaux died below the serpentine road, I happened to overhear a phone call from our Quitano," explained the inspector.

"And now guess who or what it was about, man?"

"You, Jean!" Carlos Ruiz didn't even let Jean get a word in. "You and half a million!"

"So I followed that phony Quitano, who was after you. Last night, during the shootout, I was standing about fifty meters behind you. I got rid of poor Quitano when you sped off with your wounded mutt. How's the dog, by the way? He survived, unlike our Quitano, didn't he?"

"Yes," Jean replied briefly and began to shiver.

"I still have a lot of questions," Carlos Ruiz replied calmly. "Who was Quitano really, who was that bastard on the phone with? Who does the money you're still hiding belong to? Where are the five hundred thousand? Because you never really buried it at the ruins."

"If I tell you, Inspector, what guarantee do I have that you won't kill me on the spot?"

The inspector cleared his throat. Now he looked a little offended again.

"Do you think I'm a cold-blooded killer, Señor?"

Jean shrugged.

"Listen, Inspector! I've known men who have killed for far less!"

"Calm down, Jean, let me tell you how I see it!" Ruiz began twiddling his thumbs. "The five hundred thousand euros came from blackmail and are not known to the police. Good. Brieaux probably relieved some rich guy of his money."

"It doesn't matter, because he can't do anything with the dosh anyway, dead as he is. But we're both still alive, and a quarter of a million would be a nice addition to my meager police pension, wouldn't it?"

"You're forgetting one small detail, man," Jean replied.

"Brieaux was killed by someone, and that someone wants his money. And they probably won't stop at murder."

"Listen, Jean, Quitano is our scapegoat! He took the dough and ran off somewhere. It's all thanks to me that it looks like this to the rest of the world. You just have to play along, and this will stay between us!"

"Very reassuring, Inspector, because you're not in the line of fire!"

The policeman smiled benevolently at Jean. "But I've got three weeks' vacation starting tomorrow. So I'll have plenty of time to keep an eye on you. Maybe we'll even kill two birds with one stone."

Jean Sarre knew that he currently had no other option but to agree to the corrupt inspector's terms.

The prospect of having to share his find hurt him deeply, but at least he wouldn't have to go to jail for murdering a police officer, at least not for the time being.

The only question was how far he could trust Carlos Ruiz.

The stupidest thing he could do now would probably be to walk to the hidden five hundred thousand euros with the corrupt inspector in tow.

After all, he didn't want to tempt Carlos Ruiz into doing something stupid. Despite everything, Jean had no yearning for death.

So the two men agreed that Jean would visit the detective inspector at his office that same evening.

On neutral ground, so to speak, the expert would hand over exactly half of his find to the police officer. But before Carlos Ruiz left the house, he turned back to him and grinned broadly. "I almost forgot that I brought something for you, Jean. Come out to my car for a moment!"

Jean Sarre was more than a little puzzled when the police officer opened the tailgate of his aging station wagon.

"The doc had to put a muzzle on him, but somehow he managed to free himself during the drive and licked my face at least a dozen times.

Apparently, your dog likes me, even though I was scared shitless of him. I almost had a heart attack."

Awkwardly and trembling all over, Arthos jumped out of the car in one leap. The Doberman rushed toward Jean in a zigzag pattern. Panting wildly and whimpering softly, he sought the closeness of his master. The big dog's tail wagged happily.

Jean stroked him carefully, trying not to get too close to the freshly stitched wound.

"What a tough dog!" The cop's brief remark lightened the mood.

"But how... how did you know that, Inspector?" Jean asked, looking at him questioningly.

"It's simple, Jean. Your vet got cold feet. He called me right away. When he told me the story, I was able to calm him down, thank God. By the way, Doc Vasquez is a friend of mine. So I was able to convince him not to press charges. Maybe you should have offered him a little more? In any case, you've saved twenty thousand euros of your share and, despite everything, you're not in custody. Today is your lucky day, man!"

Jean cleared his throat. The expert turned to his dog, who was noisily attacking the water bowl. Arthos swayed dazedly from side to side as he drank all the water in no time.

"Speaking of firearms!" Ruiz remarked briefly, "I've already disposed of the bullet that was lodged in your dog, but now please hand me your gun immediately before you do something stupid with it again!"

The tone of his voice had suddenly taken on an extremely demanding, interrogatory character in Jean's ears.

"By the way, where is Quitano's gun? It wasn't near his body!" The inspector began to scrutinize Jean with an extremely piercing gaze.

"I have no idea where it is. Or wait! I think I threw it somewhere in the bushes."

"And you expect me to believe that... seriously?"

"Just believe it!" whispered Jean, trying not to blush.

While Carlos Ruiz waited outside the house, Jean Sarre retrieved the Glock pistol from under the sofa. He put it in a nylon bag so he could hand it over to the police officer.

"See you tonight, amigo!" The detective inspector took the gun, got into the station wagon, and drove quickly down the street, while Jean watched him for a long time, his brow furrowed.

Arthos had drunk at least two liters of water by now. After thoroughly wetting the bushes, he had made himself comfortable on the cool floor tiles. The Doberman now needed to recover. His owner left him alone. Sarre was extremely happy to have his loyal comrade back with him.

So that young veterinarian had ratted him out after all.

"Well," he thought, "it turned out okay after all—at least luck hadn't completely turned against him."

Jean made sure he had locked the front door properly. Then he walked leisurely behind the house toward the swimming pool.

The houses next to his estate were currently unoccupied. Behind them, in the canal, there were no boats passing by.

So he took Quitano's loaded Sig Sauer pistol and the cash box from their hiding place.

Among his finds, he suddenly came across the homemade compact disc labeled "CCR-Very Best."

CCR, or Creedence Clearwater Revival, a band from the sixties or seventies that Jean also liked very much. "Proud Mary, Suzie Q., etc., etc.," more or less simple but good songs that most people found catchy.

Jean took the compact disc out of its protective case to put the silver disc into his cheap player, which was standing on the sideboard.

After loading and a short pause, "Bad Moon Rising" was the first song to play. Jean Sarre caught himself humming along to the melody.

"The song fits somehow, like a glove. Besides, it's still a full moon," he mused, still whistling the end. So he was surprised when he realized that no other song followed.

"Strange, only one song on the entire 'Best Of' CD?" He took out the disc and put it in his laptop's CD drive to check. Suddenly, the media player opened and started playing an obviously homemade video.

"Well, hello there!" Jean thought in amazement. At the same moment, he was briefly annoyed that the image was relatively blurry.

On a cheesy, heart-shaped bed lay a young man who kept running his right hand vainly through his shoulder-length dark hair. Suddenly, he jumped up, walked over to the hidden camera, and adjusted something.

Now the image quickly became clearer. Before the dandy made himself comfortable again, he dimmed the ceiling lights a little.

Shortly afterwards, a dark-haired woman appeared in the picture. She was wearing a white summer dress and stood at the head of the bed in a seductive pose. The man tried to lure the woman onto the bed. The beauty quickly took a step back and raised her index finger, laughing.

But just seconds later, she let her light dress slip to the floor and allowed her lover to pull her onto the heart-shaped bed. The young woman had a breathtaking figure. Jean Sarre leaned a little closer to the 15-inch display.

Now the two were kissing. They rolled around in different directions, pressing and writhing like two snakes entwined. Probably both had to be careful not to fall out of bed.

"Great," thought Jean, lighting a cigarette.

"Some perverted weirdo is secretly filming himself having sex with his girlfriend and burning it onto a CD!" The film continued to play quietly while he brewed himself a mega-strong espresso.

Jean smoked, drank his espresso, and stroked his dog when suddenly the whimpering started. "Damn it, what?" Jean looked at his notebook in confusion. He had turned the volume all the way down. The image changed, and not just that. It had to be a different video. Instead of the bedroom with the tacky bed, Jean could now see something that looked like an operating room. Someone must have been secretly filming with a hidden camera again, because the image was constantly shaking.

Now the camera panned to the operating tables.

Five people lay side by side in the middle of the room. They were strapped down by their arms and legs and gagged.

Nevertheless, they tried to free themselves. They twitched frantically on the shiny steel tables.

The shaky camera repeatedly showed the pitiful figures.

Jean could make out a man on the far left operating table and a woman next to him. The three other tables were occupied by smaller people, probably children.

The five appeared to be a family.

Several minutes passed. By now, the man on the left was the only one still trying to free himself.

Jean didn't like this at all. He stared intently at the notebook display while nervously tugging at his barely existent upper lip beard.

Then two more people appeared in the room and Jean tried to concentrate on the sound.

"Estupendo, I see Nurse Gerard has everything ready! Then we can get started, Nurse Rita, right?" The nurse nodded to the green-clad speaker, and at the same time, the video image shook.

First, the fat speaker with the equally thick glasses started messing with the man who was still writhing on the steel table.

"Check that the electrodes are securely attached, head nurse! I want to know what his brain waves are doing! That way we'll kill two birds with one stone. Fresh organs and pain research. Profession and vocation!

I'll have my book finished soon. You'll get the first two copies of The Wonderful World of Pain."

"Oh yes, Doctor Eugenio, you make me, the Pedro Leon Hospital, Vidasacra, indeed all of Spain, infinitely proud!"

Giggling, the nurse stepped next to the patient to get to work.

The orderly, Gerard, was still standing aside, secretly filming. Now the doctor gave some indistinct orders. His assistants then moved closer to the first operating table.

What followed was definitely not for the faint of heart.

First, Eugenio Kremer cut open the unfortunate man's abdominal wall while he was fully conscious. Blood spurted in all directions. The expert couldn't watch the carnage for long. Slightly trembling and visibly shocked, he abruptly closed the notebook. After that, he suddenly felt an urgent need to vomit right there and then.

"This can't be true, what a load of crap! Damn it ..." he said over and over to himself. Just thinking about what this sadistic doctor had done to those poor people made his stomach churn.

"Who would do something like that? And more importantly, why would someone film something like that?"

Suddenly, Jean felt like he was getting closer to the truth. The dead man, this photographer or journalist, or whatever he was. The man's name was Gerard Brieaux, GERARD! That was exactly how the nurse had addressed this fat sadist.

So Brieaux had secretly filmed this mess. He must have blackmailed them for half a million.

Five hundred thousand euros in bloody hush money.

"Damned dirty money! Most likely, the cash was obtained by selling organs!" thought Jean as he went to the cupboard to get a map.

All that money had poisoned his blood. But now it had to stop. He would have to earn the dough first! So he could put an end to this sadistic doctor and his lackeys once and for all.

"Doctor Eugenio, Pedro Leon Hospital in Vidasacra," Jean muttered a few times as he frantically searched the map.

It took a while, but then the expert found the place called 'Vidasacra' in the middle of the Pyrenees.

Jean would have to discuss the matter with the inspector. He didn't like the idea at all. After all, he could hardly do it alone. Besides, he had to find out somehow what awaited him in that hospital.

How far could he trust Carlos Ruiz?

Then he remembered that there was another video.

Was there any connection between the homemade porn and the horror film that followed?

If the Frenchman had secretly filmed both videos, who was his female actor? Did he want to blackmail the woman in the end? Although Jean had hardly slept all night, he didn't feel tired at all; rather, he was extremely pumped.

So, for a change, he made himself a cup of tea and thought about the black-haired woman. Suddenly, he saw Elena in his mind's eye and decided to call her.

After trying three times without success, he opened his notebook again to watch the first video with renewed concentration.

This time, he tried to find some clues. Who was the young woman? How far was she involved in the whole story?

Apart from the excessive moaning, Jean Sarre heard a few snippets of conversation between the wild duo.

While in the "doggy style position," the two talked incessantly, calling each other by name.

"Oh yes, come on, do it to me... harder!... you're so hard... Yes... I'm coming! ... you're filling me up... Oh yes, Gerard!"

"Oooaaah yes... Mercedes, you... I love you... I'm ready too... Almost... Dios mio!"

That was all the information that could be gleaned from the homemade film. Jean thought about it.

"Mercedes? Where had he heard that name before? Stop! The note with the phone number!"

"MF," the 'M' must be an abbreviation for the woman's name Mercedes.

After a moment's hesitation, Jean decided to simply contact this Mercedes.

After all, he had something interesting for the black-haired woman. He also hoped fervently to find out more about her.

Mercedes Falgas was very surprised, or rather slightly shocked, to receive a call from a stranger. The man on the phone refused to give his name, but he was determined to meet her to show her a video.

The film was supposed to show her acting completely naturally.

When the man hung up, Mercedes realized that the stranger hadn't mentioned a price. "Normally, blackmailers always demand money," she thought, secretly wondering how she should prepare for such a meeting.

Besides, she really couldn't figure out what the man with the unmistakable accent meant. "Maybe it's a trap. I should probably take my stun gun with me, just in case," the Catalan woman thought. Somehow, Señora Falgas felt slightly unsettled. But this afternoon, in Cadaqués, she would surely be wiser.

When Jean set off for Cadaqués at around 3 p.m., he was on tenterhooks. The old Toyota wound its way down the many curves to the quaint fishing village, and his dog insisted on accompanying him.

Jean had slept for a few hours after the short phone call, but nightmares had made for a restless night.

At first, he didn't want to take his Doberman with him. But Arthos begged so heartbreakingly that Jean simply couldn't refuse. So he drove slowly and carefully to spare his dog, who had just had surgery.

On the other hand, Arthos could also guard his notebook and his Land Cruiser while he chatted with this black-haired woman over a cup of coffee.

Yes, Jean was somehow taken with this hot-blooded Spanish woman. He had seen her in action, after all, and in his imagination he saw himself with Mercedes, lying on that cheesy heart-shaped bed. When Jean thought about that first video clip, he got an involuntary erection. But as soon as he remembered the second video, it was over. Gone was the erection, gone was the boner.

CHAPTER 7: *Cadaqués*

Jean Sarre parked the Landcruiser in the large, guarded parking lot, gave the dog some fresh water, and then set off on foot. He liked the small, picturesque alleys of the former fishing village. Stairs carved into the rocks and slate, slate, and more slate everywhere.

A real artists' village with lots of flair. Not at all like the Catalan tourist hotspots.

A few years ago, many hippies still vacationed here. Jean could remember various situations. Even in the late 1980s, you would constantly encounter stoned tourists. Pink Floyd's "Shine on Your Crazy Diamond" could be heard coming from many a guesthouse room.

But Cadaqués had also changed and, over the years, had done its best to shake off its seedy image.

Today, the tourists were wealthier. They had to be, because prices had skyrocketed here too, at least since the introduction of the euro.

Jean still had a little time, so he climbed the natural stone steps to the white, picturesque church. "A woman in high heels would probably break her ankles here," he thought, and couldn't help but grin.

When he reached the top, he stood on the church square. He sat down on the wall to enjoy the view of the whitewashed houses and down to the sea.

The smaller ships and boats anchored down in the bay briefly reminded him that he had once planned to get his boating license during his vacation. But at the same moment, he dismissed the thought and was annoyed with himself. After all, he needed his concentration for other things at the moment.

Besides, he couldn't get the song "Shine on Your Crazy Diamond" out of his head. So he whistled and hummed it quietly to himself. About three meters in front of him, a silvery coin lay on the dusty churchyard of the "Eglesia de Santa Maria."

Jean stared at it for a while, his eyes growing heavy and suddenly feeling infinitely tired. In less than an hour, he would meet Mercedes Falgas in the town center.

The two had agreed to meet in front of the casino. Well, then he could rest a little longer here on the wall.

Suddenly, an old woman dressed in raven black came out of the church. "Strange," he thought, because he could have sworn that the church door had been locked earlier.

The woman limped in his direction. Jean had the feeling that the dark eyes deep in her sunburnt face were looking right through him.

The old woman supported her small, crooked body with a wooden stick. Suddenly, she stumbled and began to lose her balance. She swayed considerably. At the same time, she began to shake violently and the stick fell from her hand.

Although Jean was tired, he jumped down from the wall. With quick reflexes, he lunged toward the old woman. At the last moment, he was able to prevent her from falling.

"Oooh... Santa Maria, muchas gracias! Young man, that was very kind of you! My old, rotten bones probably wouldn't have survived the fall onto the hard ground unscathed."

"De nada, you're welcome, grandmother," replied Jean, who found the old woman dressed in deep black somehow eerie. "Take care of yourself, good woman! I'm afraid I have to go now because I have an appointment at the casino bar."

"Jajaja, always in a hurry, young people. Go on, or no, wait a moment. Give me your left hand, señor!" Jean was a little taken aback, but he cautiously held out his left hand.

"You know, young man, my son is just as helpful as you are!" said the old woman as she searched Jean's palm with her bony, gout-ridden fingers.

"So how are things looking for me in the love department?" Jean joked.

"Love? ... You can't trust a woman you've fallen in love with or are about to fall in love with, my son!"

"Great!" he remarked wryly.

Jean felt that the hunchbacked old woman was slowly taking him for a fool. He was annoyed and wanted to pull his hand back. But his left hand was stuck, as if in a vice.

"Listen, Jean! Up in the mountains, you have the opportunity to save many lives!"

"How do you know my name?" Jean paused.

"Your blood is still poisoned, but you will free the people, I am sure of it. You may be in the process of going from Saul to Paul, but up there in the mountains, you will have to be a mixture of Saul and the Archangel Gabriel. Don't forget that!"

Jean felt hot and cold at the same time.

"Who are you?" The old woman let go of him and slowly turned away.

"Mary, my name is Mary! Please ... Please leave the silver coin!"

As the old lady walked away from him, he stood there paralyzed. "Mary, how do you know my name?" Jean wanted to call after her, but he literally choked on his own words. He wanted to follow her, wanted to ask her so many things, but he stood there, rooted to the spot.

All he could see was that the woman's gait had changed. Her limp was gone. She was walking tall. Jean shook himself, almost falling off the church wall.

He had fallen asleep. Had he just dreamed it? But the conversation with this Maria had been so real. He looked at his left hand. He couldn't see anything on his palm, but it was cold as ice.

The silvery coin was still lying in the sand in front of him. He glanced at his watch and realized that he had dozed off for almost an hour. He had to get going so he wouldn't miss Mercedes. For a moment, he considered picking up the coin. But he left it there and hurried on his way.

The casino café bar was an imposing building.

Above the CASINO sign was another inscription:

"Societat-Lámistad" – Society of Friendship.

"Lámistad – friendship!" Jean couldn't help thinking about his time in the military.

He rubbed his forehead briefly, as if to wipe away the memories, and concentrated again on what was about to happen. As soon as Jean entered the bar, he saw her sitting at a table in the corner. Sarre's pulse quickened. Why did he suddenly think of the melodrama "Casablanca"? After all, he wasn't in a black-and-white movie, and his name wasn't Rick or Humphrey. Besides, the greeting "Here's looking at you, kid!" would probably not go down too well with Señora Falgas.

The stereotypical Spaniard had a large cup of latte in front of her. Lost in thought, she took a drag on an e-cigarette. Although she was just sitting there waiting for him, Mercedes had an aura that fascinated Jean. He went straight over to her table to greet her. He held out his right hand.

"Hola, my name is Jean, nice to meet you."

"Well ... whether it's nice or not, that remains to be seen, doesn't it?" Mercedes looked at him coolly and defiantly. The Spanish woman didn't even consider shaking hands.

Jean Sarre had withdrawn his hand and simply sat down next to her. "Listen, Señora ... You could be a little friendlier to me," he said with a smile.

"Why should I be?" she replied snappishly.

"After all, you want to blackmail me with something, and you've probably already blackmailed my husband!"

Jean's expression darkened instantly.

"Nonsense, what makes you think that? I stumbled across something by chance! Maybe you can help me with it, at least I hope so."

"So you don't want any money?"

"No, I don't!"

Mercedes Falgas now became much friendlier and asked Jean if she could order him something to drink.

He smiled and said yes, so she ordered him a coffee as well.

As they sat there sipping their lattes, the two slowly struck up a conversation.

They talked about everything under the sun, about music, about Cadaqués, and, of course, about the artist Salvador Dali.

They quickly realized that they had similar tastes in music. They also shared the same views on art.

A piece of cheese was slowly going bad in the corner. For Jean and his attractive conversation partner, it had nothing to do with art.

"It's unbelievable who calls themselves an artist these days!" Mercedes remarked during the conversation.

"I completely agree with you, Señora Falgas. But Salvador Dali was an important artist. Even if he was a little crazy. But we both admit that, don't we?"

Mercedes Falgas laughed heartily. Her eyes sparkled at him. Once again, Jean felt a pleasant sensation in his loins.

Here in this area, the late artist was and remains the main attraction. The great surrealist also lived in Cadaqués for several years. The museum in Figueres was besieged by tourists from morning to night, especially during the high season. Even Jean had visited it once a few years ago.

However, he still couldn't understand why the eccentric Dali considered a box containing his wife Gala's pubic hair to be art. "Genius and madness ... the line between the two is often blurred," he philosophized. "Oh yes, Señor Sarre, you're probably right! But Dali, who was born and died in Figueres, also liked to provoke people." After this lengthy, very pleasant conversation, Mercedes began to grow impatient.

"So, Jean, what's the deal with this video?"

"A little patience," he replied.

"Listen, let's finish our lattes. Then we'll go to my car together. I have my laptop in there, and we can watch the videos on it."

"The videos?" Mercedes Falgas raised her eyebrows.

"By the way, did anyone follow you?"

"Not that I'm aware of," she replied.

"Good, then let's go!"

After Mercedes paid the bill, Jean led the Catalan woman to his car.

On the way there, he noticed a few male gazes. Oh yes, Mercedes Falgas, née Leon, was truly a breathtakingly beautiful woman.

Jean could already imagine what the men were thinking as they looked enviously at the unlikely couple.

When they arrived at the parking lot, Jean advised the black-haired woman to stay back a few meters. "Wait a moment, I'll just let my dog out of the car." Arthos barked briefly when he saw the two of them coming.

"Go ahead, I'm not afraid of dogs."

As soon as the door was open, the black-and-tan dog jumped out of the car. The Doberman greeted the two of them enthusiastically.

Mercedes Falgas slowly knelt down to let Arthos sniff her a little before gently stroking him.

"He's a handsome fellow, but where did he get that injury?"

"Oh, don't ask, Mercedes. Anyway, it has something to do with all the trouble I've gotten myself into!"

Jean took the notebook out of the car and opened it. Mercedes came over to him, interested. She was astonished when the first video played on the media player.

"That damn... I had no idea... that bastard ... that asshole Gerard just used me!"

Mercedes's face turned from sun-kissed to ashen. But it was about to get even better.

"Turn that off, Jean!" Mercedes wanted to throw the notebook against the wall, but instead she contented herself with closing the display.

"Hey, wait, I want you to watch the second film too!"

"I've seen enough!" Mercedes replied defiantly.

"Listen, Mercedes, have a smoke first and calm down. Then watch the other film, okay?"

Mercedes nodded hesitantly.

After watching the second film, the young woman completely lost her composure.

"That damn Eugenio Kremer. What is he doing? What in God's name is he doing to those poor people? That madman! That monster!" Mercedes began to sob loudly.

Completely distraught and pale as a ghost, she pressed herself tightly against Jean. Like a little child who wants to cry on her father's shoulder.

At least that's how it seemed to Jean at first. But the embrace, especially the way she pressed herself against him, didn't just awaken Jean's protective instincts.

Her tears stained his light blue shirt dark.

Mercedes told Jean about Vidasacra. Now the words just poured out of her. But she spoke softly. She still sobbed from time to time.

Jean had to concentrate hard to make head or tail of it. The story began with her father, who had the hospital built back then, and ended with snippets of conversation she had picked up at some point.

Her husband and this Doctor Kremer; both were involved in some shady dealings, but she had known that for a long time.

Mercedes had also noticed in previous years that her husband had received a tip from a high-ranking official about an impending raid. Unfortunately, she couldn't remember whether the tipster was a police officer or a prosecutor.

In any case, her husband had excellent contacts. This enabled the construction magnate to hide the illegal workers in the hospital before the authorities discovered the illegal employment. But what did that sadistic doctor do to the Colombian workers and their families? Was her husband really aware of these unspeakable acts of brutality? It was hard to imagine!

But the way her "Juanito" had changed in recent years... The second film, that horror movie, would probably stay with her forever. Suddenly, the homemade porn lost all its importance. Nevertheless, she couldn't help thinking about her former lover. The young woman felt something like shame.

Gerard Brieaux, that blackmailing bastard.

Now he was dead! But she had cried for this damned man for nothing. He had promised her the moon, laid her on a bed of roses, and yet he had only used and betrayed her.

Mercedes looked at Jean with the saddest eyes he had seen in a long time. She flicked her half-smoked Marlboro away in a high arc.

"Unbelievable. I'm so sorry!"

"What are you sorry for?" Jean asked, somewhat confused.

"That I lost control for a moment earlier. But I'm fine now, I promise!"

Arthos was also a little perplexed. Especially by the fact that this strange woman had given his master such an adrenaline rush.

He lay behind the Toyo and watched the scene with great interest.

"No problem, you don't need to apologize, Mercedes. Really!

Calm down! Drive home now. We'll talk on the phone later. Give me a call or just drop by.

Just don't talk to anyone about this, okay?"

The young woman understood. After they had both agreed that Mercedes must maintain absolute silence, especially towards her husband, the two parted ways.

But first they arranged a second meeting.

In the meantime, Mercedes was to keep her eyes and ears open. Hopefully, she might even be able to secure some clues or evidence.

Señora Falgas got into a black Porsche Boxster, which she had parked by chance not far from Jean's Toyota. She started the six-cylinder engine, waved briefly to him, and then sped toward the gate, which opened immediately.

Jean also slowly made his way out of the parking lot. After all, he had to meet with the inspector that evening.

On the drive from Cadaqués to Empuriabrava, he had a few thoughts.

"Why does this always happen to me?"

The last few years in particular had repeatedly placed Jean in extremely precarious situations.

As Sarre drove past the Empuriabrava sports airport, a plane was taking off, transporting skydivers to dizzying heights.

The girls and boys up there must have had an incredible view. The weather was good, the blue sky almost cloudless. Maybe Jean should try it sometime. Maybe he would get a better perspective, a better overview.

However, he quickly dismissed the idea. The expert was quite afraid of heights. He started to tremble when he was on a ladder three meters above the ground.

"Damn coward," he thought aloud, annoyed with himself once again.

Although he had seen and experienced so much crap over the last few years, he was still the cautious Jean Sarre. A man approaching fifty who carried a lot of fears with him.

Slowly, he had to come to terms with the fact that, in his old age, he was anything but a brave daredevil. Damn it, Jean Sarre just wanted a quiet life.

And now ... he was supposed to... commit some kind of heroic deed to free some people.

On the other hand, he had often been in dangerous situations in the past.

It was the daredevils and the brave who had fallen in droves. One or two "tough fighters" had whimpered like children after being shot in the stomach before dying in his arms.

As he drove down his street in Falconera, cold sweat beaded on his forehead.

Jean was terrified of what lay ahead. Oh yes... but he had to get through it!

When he got home, he made himself spaghetti again and thought too much. Had it been smart to involve Mercedes Falgas? But who else could he have asked?

How many people were being held in Vidasacra?

He didn't know. What was happening up there? He had no idea.

So he took his laptop to surf the internet. He scoured all the search engines, hoping to find out more. Vidasacra... Hospital... Pedro Leon Clinic.

Two hours later, Jean entered the dark blue police station in Roses.

In the backpack he carried on his shoulders was a plastic bag containing 250,000 euros, meticulously counted.

This time, the "receptionist" was different.

At that moment, Jean wondered how the inspector had disposed of Quitano's body. But he didn't really want to know.

"How can I help you?" The smiling police officer asked Jean politely. Once again, he was nothing like the unfriendly, grumpy Quitano he had killed with his own hands.

In the next few minutes, Jean learned that Inspector Carlos Ruiz had already left for his well-deserved vacation. "If you are Jean Sarre, I have a message for you from the inspector!"

The young police officer handed him a letter.

Sarre thanked him and said goodbye, going outside to open the envelope. The inspector wanted to meet with him tomorrow evening.

CHAPTER 8: *Unprofessional*

When Jean arrived back in Empuriabrava, he immediately saw the black Golf GTI parked in front of his gate. His mood improved within milliseconds.

When he parked his old Toyota next to the Volkswagen, he saw her waving at him. "What could a classy woman like her want with a man who has lost the plot like me?" But now, he couldn't and didn't want to think about that. Right now, he just needed her shoulder. Maybe her tenderness could give him the energy he would soon need so badly. "Hola Cariño!" Elena hugged him and gave him a long kiss. "Oh, it almost feels like you really missed me!"

Elena flashed her most charming smile and Jean beamed back at her.

"Let's go inside, or no, wait a minute until my dog has met you. You're not afraid, are you?"

No sooner said than done, Arthos came rushing over. After sniffing the blonde a little, they entered Sarre's house. Shortly afterwards, they shut the bedroom door in the poor dog's face.

"Cute little dog," Elena remarked, but Jean didn't answer her, instead throwing her onto the bed.

"Well, my sweetie, you're really hungry. Wait a minute... oh, please... I want to freshen up a little first... heeeh... I'm already all... what are you doing to me?"

Jean didn't give Elena any time. Not to freshen up in the bathroom first, not for a cigarette, not for anything else.

This time was different. This time was wild and hard. This time, neither of them needed foreplay.

It was all about the quick, animalistic satisfaction of their urges.

Jean paused imperceptibly, slowing the frequency of his thrusts a little as he watched the dead Frenchman's homemade porn video in his mind's eye.

They climaxed almost simultaneously, and as the two lay silently next to each other, Jean Sarre sensed that something was wrong.

"What's wrong with you?" Elena asked at some point.
"It was very nice, but somehow... what's wrong with you?"
"Later," he replied quietly. "Let's just lie here for a few more minutes!"
Half an hour later, they were sitting on the terrace. Sarre served his new girlfriend hot coffee.
"That's a good idea! You seem to instinctively know what I need right now." Elena winked, rolled her eyes, and they both had to laugh.
Then he stood up and stripped down.
"You don't want to do that again, do you?" Elena made a horrified face for fun.

Jean grinned and ran past her deck chair. Shortly after, he jumped into the swimming pool.
"Come on, let's splash around a bit, it'll be nice and cool," he called to her, and Elena didn't need to be asked twice.
They swam, laughed, and kissed. They felt their bodies in the cool water. Jean suddenly felt energetic again.
Elena had arrived at just the right time.
After a home-cooked dinner—this time Jean had outdone himself once again with his Mediterranean spaghetti—the two sat on the pool terrace for a while and drank wine.

"We're sitting here in Spain, drinking South African Pinotage from the discount store, not bad, right?" Elena remarked roguishly.
"Well, the main thing is that it tastes good ... right?"
Jean grinned, picked up his wine glass, and clinked glasses with Elena.

"Salud, my beauty!" 'Salud."
"Yes, health is definitely the most important thing, don't you think?"
"Well, health... says the person who smokes one cigarette after another,' Elena remarked pointedly.
"Yes, okay, but everyone has to be allowed a vice or two. But I promise you, I'll cut back on my coffin nails a little ..."
'What? ... Please finish what you were saying, my darling!"
"... reduce them!"
"Just give up smoking and kiss me instead!' They both had to laugh, and Jean kissed her tenderly. But Elena noticed that something was bothering Jean.
"Why are you so serious today, Jean? Something happened, didn't it? Something's wrong with you. Don't you love me anymore? Talk to me!"
Jean Sarre desperately searched for some excuse, but perhaps it would be good to show Elena this horror spectacle. After all, he didn't have to tell her in detail how he had gotten hold of this CD.
"All right! I received a compact disc in the mail. Tomorrow I'm going to turn it over to the police!"
"Hmmm... and what's on it?" Elena's curiosity was written all over her face.
Jean told her about the CCR song and the two videos. Elena wouldn't let up until he had played the films for her.
"Damn, I didn't know that!" Elena had tears in her eyes.
"What didn't you know... I don't understand?"
"That someone could do something so terrible. How can someone revel in other people's pain?"

"That sadistic pig!"

"Oh yes, that pig. You're acting as if you know this fat pseudo-doctor!"

"Nonsense, speaking of knowing, do you know the black-haired woman in the previous film?"

Elena quickly got the hang of it.

"You've been with her before, haven't you?"

"Nonsense, what do you take me for?" said Jean with a grin.

"No, of course not, but the man who shot the two videos probably has!"

"He's a lucky guy, with that superwoman... don't you think?" The Russian woman had that innocent look on her face again.

"Well, lucky guy ..." Jean looked Elena in the eyes.

"I wouldn't necessarily call him that. The lucky guy is dead!"

After the two had talked about the videos for a while and Elena slowly spread her wings after the second bottle of red wine, Jean took her to bed and lay down next to his new girlfriend, feeling tipsy.

He lay awake for ten minutes, wondering whether it had really been a good idea to show her the videos. "Well, more people will have to see the mess," he thought. Then he fell into a restless sleep.

About two hours later, Elena Lokova carefully slipped out of bed. She had to be damn careful because Jean was tossing and turning in his sleep. "Poor darling, your bad dreams will soon be over!" thought the Russian woman as she opened her black handbag. In the semi-darkness, she took a small pistol out of her bag and screwed a cylindrical object onto it. With this silencer, not even his dog would notice anything about his master's abrupt demise. Yes, the moonlight made everything easier. In the glow of the full moon, she didn't need any additional light sources.

"How do you know so much? Cariño, Disculpe... lo siento mucho... I'm very sorry, but it has to be done!"

The blonde woman quietly loaded the handy 9mm pistol and slowly approached the sleeping man.

At that very moment, Jean Sarre began to talk in his sleep.

"Oooooh Elena, I love you ... I love you too ... so much ... Elena!"

She hadn't expected that at all in this situation. She had never been thrown off balance by a "hit" before. Her right arm began to tremble. She suddenly felt as if she were fighting off a chill, and then her professionalism crumbled.

Completely irritated, with cold sweat on her forehead, she relaxed her weapon, put it back in her bag, and left the room.

After Elena quietly closed the bedroom door behind her, she took a piece of paper out of her handbag. Still trembling, she clumsily wrote a few words on it.

To make matters even more difficult, she had to pet Jean's dog while she was writing.

Arthos had come wobbling over, half asleep, and demanded his cuddles right then and there.

After all, they could have let him sleep, and besides... where had that big, juicy veal bone disappeared to? He had just been dreaming about it!

When Sarre woke up around 7 a.m., his girlfriend was long gone. At first he thought she had just popped out for a moment—maybe to get some bread rolls—but then he found the note.

"Dear Jean, Please don't wait for me or look for me. I'm not worth it! I have to leave urgently to do something important. Thank you for opening my eyes. You are a very special person. Have a wonderful life, health, happiness, and success—Elena."

Please don't trust anyone, be careful, and leave Catalonia soon.

PS: I'm afraid something will happen to you!!!

Sarre read the note a few times. The expert couldn't make head nor tail of it.

Nervously, he dialed Elena's number again and again. But the line was constantly busy.

Restless, with a sinking feeling in the pit of his stomach, Jean Sarre paced back and forth in his house. How could this be? For the first time in a long time, he felt like he had found a woman with whom he could imagine a future. And then this.

Well, he thought, it just wasn't meant to be. Who can understand women?

It was probably better this way anyway. He told himself this over and over again. Because losing Elena right now hurt like hell, even if he didn't want to admit it.

Since Jean Sarre couldn't figure out why, how, or what had gone wrong again, he had to distract himself somehow. So he put his dog on a leash and went to get some bread rolls. He didn't have to walk too far, because there was a large campsite with a small supermarket across the street from Falconera. He might as well have stayed home, because he hadn't been feeling very hungry that morning.

In the small shop, which had just opened, he bought four rolls, a carton of Lucky Strikes, and a Catalan daily newspaper. Arthos waited patiently outside the building. Even a poodle strutting past didn't distract the Doberman.

Back home, he first made himself a strong coffee and forced himself to eat a roll with cheese. With his mouth full, he opened the newspaper. He almost had a coughing fit when he saw a photo.

"Ambulance crashes into river."

"Vidasacra Hospital Pedro Leon... Chief Physician Dr. E. Kremer reported that an ambulance was stolen. The vehicle was not missed until the next day, when it was recovered from the river. There is still no trace of the thief. There were no injuries or fatalities. The police have since closed their investigation." The clinic management had also repeatedly reminded its employees to lock their parked vehicles properly... etc.

So it was all real. This Dr. Kremer smiled at him kindly from the newspaper. Who else but Mercedes, Elena, and him knew what was going on in Vidasacra? The police... various politicians...? Jean had no idea, but sooner or later he would find out.

The detective inspector sat down at a table from which he could keep an eye on the restaurant entrance. No sooner had he sat down than he realized that his stomach was rumbling. Oh yes, he was ravenous and also extremely thirsty. So he waved to a waitress to order "UNA CERVEZA GRANDE" and fresh white bread with aioli as a starter, so to speak.

Since Carlos Ruiz was a regular here, he didn't have to worry about the bill anyway. Not long ago, he had helped the Italian restaurant owner out of a tight spot. Since then, he had generally been drinking and eating for free.

Ruiz was quite excited. Somehow, his current mood was a mixture of nervousness and elation. This intensified when he saw the appraiser enter.

Jean Sarre looked around, the inspector made himself known, and the insurance employee purposefully weaved his way past several tables full of tourists.

"Hola Señor Sarre; nice to see you!"

The policeman motioned Jean to sit down with a sweeping gesture.

"Well, do you have it with you, I hope...?"

Carlos Ruiz looked at Jean with a pointedly questioning expression.

"Claro, Inspector," Sarre replied with a pained smile, wondering why Ruiz raised his eyebrows so dramatically when he asked the question.

He handed the backpack to the policeman and secretly felt very annoyed. But the man would have to continue earning his money. The mere thought of that eased the pain of losing a quarter of a million.

Carlos Ruiz opened the backpack, glanced inside, and then set it down next to his chair. Then he rubbed his hands together contentedly, smiled broadly, and called the restaurant manager over. The manager was a small, bald man with glasses. He came running over promptly. When Carlos stood up to greet him, the man seemed almost intimidated.

"Bring my friend everything he wants and put it on my tab, jefe ... oh, what the heck ... first bring us the best bottle of champagne you have! We have something to celebrate! Right, Señor Sarre?"

Jean was somewhat taken aback, more or less awkward, and wondered what kind of drugs the inspector had taken for breakfast. Meanwhile, the bald man with glasses walked away from their table without saying a word. "Listen, Ruiz. Calm down, and above all, don't make a scene! You got what you wanted. Now control yourself, because the tourists over there are already getting thick-skinned. Besides, we need to talk!" "What do you mean, Sarre... Can't I even enjoy my windfall? Why so serious, my friend? What's on your mind?"

"Wait until we've eaten, Inspector. Otherwise you'll lose your appetite!"

"Go ahead, man! I'm already full anyway. Too much bread with aioli... well then." The cop grinned, and in the meantime the champagne was served.

Jean looked at him seriously. Disgruntled, he began to report to the inspector. In a subdued voice, focused and without any emotion, he described the situation to the police officer.

He told him about the compact disc, about the Colombians who had been killed in the Vidasacra hospital, about Kremer, the entrepreneur Falgas... but he left out Mercedes.

Inspector Ruiz was visibly shaken; at least, that was the impression he gave. "Mierda, damn it! Then our shared money is blood money, in the truest sense of the word, isn't it?" said the police officer dramatically. He rubbed his nose nervously.

During the conversation, Ruiz promised that he would personally put an end to the bloody goings-on. He repeatedly asserted that it didn't matter to him who was involved.

Why did Jean have the stupid feeling that he was just being reassured? Somehow, the policeman made a strange impression on the expert.

"By the way, where do you have the evidence? You know what I mean... that CD! I need it before I can do anything! Did you leave it at home?"

"No," replied Jean. "It's in my notebook, which is in my car!"

"Okay, okay... listen, Jean. I need to take a quick bathroom break. After we eat, we'll go to your car together. Then you give me that disc and I'll take care of everything else! This is police work, do you understand me?"

Jean raised his eyebrows as he nodded. At the same time, Carlos Ruiz had already gotten up and was on his way to the restroom. At the same time, a waiter brought the food they had ordered.

Jean sat alone at the table and thought. Actually, he could be satisfied. Now he had the police on the case. The guys should take care of this pseudo-hospital. He would hand the CD over to the inspector. Everything else was none of his business. "One less thing to worry about!" he thought. Why did his gut feeling tell him something completely different?
When the inspector returned to the table, he tried to smile painfully. "Is something wrong, Inspector?" Jean had just started eating his pizza.
"No, Señor Sarre, but these damn hemorrhoids are killing me!"
Jean tried to smile sympathetically. "Well... we all have our crosses to bear! Now sit down, Inspector Ruiz, or your food will get cold. That would be a shame, wouldn't it?"
Although both men had completely lost their appetite, they tried to hide this fact from each other.
"Good, isn't it?" "Yes... very tasty. I haven't eaten this well in a long time! The Quattro Queso is fantastic!"
Shortly afterwards, a teenager entered the restaurant. The black-haired boy was carrying a large bouquet of red roses under his arm. He headed straight for the table where Ruiz and Sarre were eating.
"Why is he coming over to us?" thought Jean. The rose seller simply ignored the English, French, Italian, and

German customers. The boy stood in front of their table, looking questioningly.

"Hola y Adiós, Chico!" the inspector remarked dryly. The policeman didn't even look up from his lasagna.

"Buenas Tardes, Señores. Would you like to buy a rose?"

The black-haired boy looked questioningly at Jean Sarre.

"No, Gracias," Jean replied curtly.

"Then I'll give you one!" replied the teenager.

Jean had to laugh out loud. The inspector continued eating without showing any reaction. "All right, kid. Do what you gotta do! But you've got it all wrong. You're supposed to sell the flowers, not give them away! If I were at least a pretty blonde ... then I could understand you." He continued laughing.

Only now did Jean notice that the rose seller kept glancing toward the entrance.

"Gracias y Adiós, Señores." The boy wrapped a long-stemmed rose in a piece of paper. He quickly threw it on the table in front of Jean. Confused, the appraiser looked at the beautiful flower.

He wanted to ask the boy what the point of it all was, but he was already leaving the restaurant at a brisk pace.

Carlos Ruiz also looked up. The police officer examined the red rose with interest.

He slowly unwrapped the paper and smoothed it out on the table.

Someone had written something on it in shaky handwriting. It was difficult to read, but unmistakable.

Seconds later, there was a deafening bang in front of the restaurant.

The shock wave shattered the two large windows in the entrance area. The door was thrown toward the center of the room. There was screaming everywhere, pure chaos!

A woman sitting perhaps two meters away from Jean's table held her head with both hands. Glass shards had cut her face. Jean had also been hit by something. A piece of window frame had struck his right arm. He was bleeding...

"Mierda!" The inspector stood up from the floor, cursing, his backpack in his hand, and pulled Jean with him.

Passing by restaurant guests who were crying, whimpering, or screaming, the two men staggered through the large hole that had recently been the entrance door.

Outside, Jean just stared at the spot where he had parked his Land Cruiser. There was smoke and fire everywhere!

"I must be dreaming!" he thought. "This is all just a nightmare, wake up!"

But the sight of the burning wreck that had once been his car brought him back to the sad reality.

"Arthos, Arthos ... AAAAArthos ...?!

Jean was beside himself.

"I'm sorry!" Carlos Ruiz put his hand on the expert's shoulder, but he turned away and walked apathetically toward the flames.

CHAPTER 9: *Desire for revenge*

About three hours later, a completely distraught man sat alone in the darkness of his home. He had lost a good friend that evening. Full of self-reproach and with tears in his eyes, Jean kept looking at his dog's favorite spot. There stood the stand with the two metal bowls. There was still a little water left in the right bowl. Sarre had been so happy that the Doberman had survived the gunshot wound, but now his dog was dead... torn apart by an explosive device.

"Damn it, why... why?" thought Sarre, rummaging in his pants pocket and pulling out the crumpled piece of paper. The fake rose seller had been shitting himself when he delivered the message to Jean.

Jean stared at the battered piece of paper for a long time. He read the message over and over again. He wiped the tears from his eyes, becoming more aggressive by the second. He wasn't going to let himself be driven away so easily. Besides, it wasn't just about the money anymore. He wasn't going to cower in front of those cowardly bombers. He was going to kick their asses, and he was almost certain that it would happen in Vidasacra.

So many memories ran through his mind. Only after half a bottle of Osborne 103 did he feel the necessary heaviness. Somewhere, the Ramones were playing a familiar song.

"I wanna be sedated!" That was exactly what he needed right now.

Sure, Sarre knew that the bright amber-colored brandy wouldn't solve his problems, but it would calm him down tonight and hopefully help him sleep.

Eventually, he fell asleep on the leather couch in the living room. The only light came from a small, old-fashioned lamp with a lampshade that he had placed on a side table. It wasn't a bad idea, because if he had to get up quickly to go to the bathroom tonight, at least he wouldn't be standing in complete darkness in his drunken state.

Jean Sarre had bad dreams. His subconscious replayed the events of the past few days.

Drenched in sweat, he slowly but surely stuck to the couch. Then suddenly, towards morning, there was a knock at the front door.

The expert was startled, slowly got up, and staggered through his living room. He tripped over the empty brandy bottle and fell flat on his face.

"Mierda, damn it! Who is it? ... Come in!" Jean clumsily got back on his feet and staggered to the front door.

Outside stood an unkempt guy who looked like he'd been through hell.

"I need to talk to you ... You have to help me, man!" the guy almost begged. "They killed my brother in that fucking hospital! Now those bastards are after me!"

Jean was instantly sober. The unshaven man with jet-black, greasy hair looked up at him. Afterwards, he wondered what the hell had possessed him to invite him in with a wave of his hand.

"Why are you coming to me? Why don't you go to the police? Who are you anyway?"

Sarre felt taken aback. At the same time, however, his curiosity grew, and he asked the Spaniard one question after another.

During the conversation, which was interrupted by many pauses, one thing became clear. Jean Sarre quickly realized what had motivated the burglar to target his former victim.

"The enemy of my enemy must be my friend!"

The two men then realized that they had at least some common goals.

Revenge, or rather putting an end to the goings-on in Vidasacra, would make them accomplices. Jean also knew that having a burglar on board couldn't be a disadvantage, at least.

"Okay, Señor Pascal, it's a deal... I'll put on a pot of coffee. Then we'll have breakfast first."

Pascal nodded happily and smiled broadly, revealing his rotten teeth for a moment.

Slowly, the mistrust disappeared. After the insurance agent and the petty criminal had regained their strength, their conversation continued.

Pascal told Jean what he had experienced in Vidasacra. Sarre let him talk and listened intently for quite some time.

In between, Jean lit a Lucky. Immediately afterwards, he offered one to his companion.

When Pascal told him about his client, a chill ran down his spine.

"A tall, blonde woman...?" Jean turned pale.

Pascal quickly understood. He told him how the attractive blonde had first contacted him and his brother. He also told him about her plan to create a diversion during the break-in.

"Shame on you, man, and you really thought?" Pascal almost blushed. "She played you... I feel sorry for you!"

"Save your pity!" Jean reacted somewhat irritably, and rightly so.

"I'm such a fool, I really thought... well... you know what, Pascal." "What?"

"Do you know what disappointment means, mate? Actually, disappointment isn't a bad thing, it's more of a positive thing!

It means that you were deceived before and now you know the truth!"

"But it still hurts, doesn't it?" Pascal took a deep breath.

"So this Elena, or whatever her real name is, is involved in this too. Well, estupendo! I trusted this woman, I even poured my heart out to her!"

"Not just your heart, right?" Pascal Cortez grinned maliciously, and Jean tried to ignore the verbal jab, but he didn't really succeed. Because he quickly became loud.

"Why don't you go to the police and tell them all this shit!"

"Okay, okay, okay... it's fine, man, sorry for the stupid comment."

"Listen, you know as well as I do that some of them are in on it. That means we can't trust anyone!"

"You're probably right, hombre! Those sons of bitches will kill us as soon as they get us," Jean replied.

"Cheer up, man! We will, or rather, we must get to them first ... espero, I hope so!"

While Pascal was showering, Jean was thinking.

He had told the burglar that Inspector Ruiz now had both the money and everything else from the find. Hopefully, Pascal wouldn't find the hiding place easily. But maybe it wouldn't be a bad idea to put the Sig Sauer under the couch now.

Who knew what would happen next!

After he had done that, with the shower still running, he laid some of his clothes in front of the bathroom door.

Pascal looked a little funny in his pants. Jean had to grin as he tossed him a can of beer. The T-shirt fit reasonably well, but the Spaniard had to roll up his pants several times.

"Gracias, amigo... you'll get your stuff back today... Jean, I promise! You could drive me to my apartment in Figueres later... Okay?" Pascal's face turned red. "Mierda, you don't have a car anymore!"

"No problem, man, but I still have a motorcycle, and we'll be faster on that anyway!"

"Forget it, I'd rather take the stolen Vespa I parked three streets away."

Who would be looking for a twenty-year-old, totally dented Vespa ... not a soul.

Pascal laughed, drank his beer, and told Sarre under what circumstances, but also and above all how, he had come here from Vidasacra.

Then he told the German about the hospital's security technology. The real problem was the security, those damn guards... How the hell were they going to get past them?

If anything, they would have to use a back exit. But the emergency exit, or rather the door he had used with that unfortunate Colombian, could only be opened from the inside. "Maybe someone can open this back door for us," said Jean, taking a sip of beer and grinning broadly.

Pascal paused and made a dismissive gesture.

"Oh, come on, mate! Do you want to get someone arrested or something? They'd probably be taken apart faster than you can blink. Or... what?"

Jean was still smiling knowingly, and that was exactly what irritated the Spaniard.

"Well...," Sarre began slowly, "the wife of the hospital's biggest donor, Señora Mercedes Falgas, will open the gates for us.

At least, I hope so! After all, she knows that damn butcher and can get through the front entrance without any problems.

What do you think, Pascal?"

"Listen, Jean... Who knows about this... Who have you told about the mess in Vidasacra?"

Pascal looked at him reproachfully and answered his own question. "So... the cop, that blonde... that Señora Falgas ... damn it ... who else?"

"No one else!" Jean replied curtly.

"Good... bien... muy bien, espero, mi amigo... espero!"

Pascal ran his fingers through his greasy hair and began to chew on his fingernails.

"Listen, Jean... I've made up my mind!"

The expert looked at him curiously.

"If you don't help me, I'll storm that damn fortress in the mountains myself. I owe it to my brother and the Colombian who took a bullet for me! I had no choice but to leave the poor devil behind. But I'm less concerned about the unfortunate people who are simply being butchered. I have to kill my brother's murderer, do you understand?"

Before Jean could answer, his cell phone rang. With a long, annoyed groan, he picked it up from the table and answered in a more or less gruff tone. "Yes... Sarre!"

On the other end of the line, there was a brief silence.

Shortly thereafter, he recognized the delicate tone of Mercedes Falgas. Jean's voice immediately became much warmer and friendlier.

"Hola, Jean. Are you okay? I heard about the explosion and was very worried! Listen... my husband is away on business... I've given my domestic staff the day off.

If you like, I can pick you up at your place. Then we can talk in peace. That is, if you want?"

There wasn't much for the expert to think about.

He agreed with a warm feeling in the pit of his stomach after politely thanking her.

She would come by in the late afternoon. That would give him the whole evening to persuade the pretty Spanish woman to help him.

"Well...?" Pascal's curiosity was written all over his face.

"Let's go, amigo! Tonight I'll try to get Señora Falgas to help us, Pascal."

The thief looked skeptical.

"Listen, Pascal... You can't do this alone... we'll do it together... that's the only way it will work... okay?"

The man with the greasy hair nodded hesitantly as he lit another cigarette.

In the afternoon, Pascal left the house at number 22 on Falconera Street. He strolled over to the old motor scooter he had parked a few streets away that morning and drove straight to his apartment in Figueres.

Extremely cautious and nervous, he crept into the musty hallway. He had to assume that they were after him. Pascal had no idea that his pursuers had long since given up the chase.

In their opinion, the brazen thief had drowned in the torrent. Even if he hadn't, he posed no great danger to them. The scoundrel would hardly go to the police.

Jean had given him a cell phone and a charger so they could stay in touch.

After packing some of his clothes into an old bag, the Spaniard left his apartment.

The expert had reluctantly lent him a thousand euros after Pascal assured him he wouldn't do a bunk with the money.

Near the Salvador Dali Museum, an old acquaintance of the Cortez brothers ran a small, run-down bistro. Almost every evening, most of the area's failed existences gathered there. It was not uncommon for several hundred years of prison time, i.e., all the burglars, thugs, and pimps in the region, to come together at the bar. Probably mainly because the boss himself was anything but a blank slate.

Señor Luca was definitely the criminal underworld mayor of Figueres. The sixty-year-old had enjoyed this role for years.

When Pascal entered the dingy bistro, he breathed a audible sigh of relief. Luckily, the establishment was still empty at this hour. Luca was just initiating a young girl into the secrets of gastronomy. The chubby waitress was trying her hand at washing glasses. Her boss was meticulously making sure she didn't use too much precious water.

The result was, of course, as expected. But at least they had both shown good will. The man from the local health authority was someone Luca helped financially from time to time anyway.

"Hola, cabrón! Well, ... Pascal. You bandit, it's good to see you again!" The tall innkeeper smiled wolfishly and held out his right hand in greeting. The thief shook it vigorously.

"Hey Luca, how's it going, dude?"

"Muy bien, muchacho, how's your little brother Fernando? Come on... let's have a drink, man!"

Luca whistled through his teeth. At the same time, he waved to his barmaid.

"Jolanda... stop cleaning! Bring us two large espressos and a bottle of cognac!"

The men chatted and laughed about trivial matters while the young woman fumbled with the coffee machine.

"You know, Pascal. There's nothing better in the afternoon than a large Carahillo; except maybe a blowjob, hahaha!"

When Luca realized that Jolanda was completely overwhelmed by the task of making coffee, he stood up abruptly and pushed his employee aside.

"Fuck you!"

"Stop raping that machine. Make yourself useful, chica!

Play with my colleague's crown jewels a little, maybe you'll get that right at least!"

The girl looked at Luca with big, sad eyes. At that moment, she didn't understand anything anymore.

"Que? What? What game? What jewels?"

The choleric boss was now on the verge of exploding, yelling even louder at his bewildered waitress.

"Go to Pascal, take his best piece and blow him, you stupid cow! Do your customer a favor... if you can't serve tapas."

As if hypnotized, the girl moved toward Pascal, knelt in front of him, and wordlessly set about the task she had been assigned.

Now it was Pascal's turn to turn red.

He slowly slid down in the small club chair. The Spaniard carefully stroked Jolandas' curly head with both hands.

"Feels good, huh? Relax ... in a few minutes I'll have our Carahillos ready!"

The landlord had put on his wolfish grin again after taking two dusty glass cups from a shelf. Then he cut a lemon and placed a bottle of Osborne Veterano in front of him. He took his time. In Lucas' opinion, a good Carahillo always consisted of an espresso, milk, lots of sugar, a quarter slice of lemon, and a good shot of brandy. Above all, the proportions had to be right, and of course it had to be served hot.

The hulking man had been dressed in black leather since his youth and prison days, was tattooed from head to toe, and had his silver-gray hair tied back in a ponytail. Luca was particularly fond of long-stroke Harley-Davidson motorcycles, five of which he owned.

He also loved flamenco music and the British band Deep Purple. That was the only explanation for the old jukebox in the corner, which mainly played Ian Gillan and Paco de Lucia.

Smoke on the Water was playing for the hundred thousandth time ... Luca sang along loudly to the chorus as usual and played air guitar.

Then the landlord took a small gray tray and placed the two Carahillos on it. Now he strutted over to Pascal's table with his head held high. Jolanda was still busy under the table, but now she was cleaning up.

Pascal had just zipped up his pants, grinning like a Cheshire cat.

"Relax ... Relaxing ... huh?" Lucas's throaty laugh filled the entire room.

"Bien ... muy bien ... estupendo!"

"So ... nice for you, amigo."

Luca lit a cigarette, reached under the table, and pulled his staff member out from underneath it by her hair. He was a brutal guy and a mean pimp, but she didn't complain.

None of his girls would ever complain and get away with it. The boss stroked her cheek, ordered her to get up and smoke one outside the bar. The young woman stood up and took the three filter cigarettes Luca held out to her. Then she went outside without saying a word.

The two men drank their coffee. Luca was once again enjoying his role as the selfless patron.

"Well, how do you like my Carahillo especial?" asked the bartender. 'Damn good!' replied Pascal with a smile.

"But the appetizer wasn't too shabby either!"

The two laughed.

"If you want, you can fuck Jolanda later. But that'll cost you, amigo... understand!"

"Aha... that's how you do things!" Pascal quipped.

"First you hook someone up. Then you do your deal... clever, clever!"

"Claro amigo, esta la vida, esta la guerra... You know I'm a businessman. Besides, I figured you liked big butts!" Luca held his stomach with laughter.

"Maybe you're right, but that's not why I'm here. I need your help, Luca!"

Pascal told his story while his counterpart listened attentively. Until it burst out of him.

"Damn... and that doctor just put our Fernando
in the oven alive... really?"

The thief nodded and continued talking to the landlord.

"Mierda! What are you telling me... and what do you think I should do, mate?

There's no money to be made in this business. So what do you want?"

"You'd do the same, Luca!

I need two sharp guns and the ammunition to go with them."

The landlord sighed, slowly rubbing his graying temples.

"No problem, but it'll be your expense!" Pascal waved him off. He reached into his pocket to put a thousand euros on the table in front of Luca.

"Do me a favor, because that's all I've got. Do it for Nando!"

Luca looked him deep in the eyes and took a drag on a cigarette that was almost burned down to the filter.

He slowly stood up, winked encouragingly at Pascal as he pocketed the money. Then the giant disappeared into his bistro kitchen.

A few minutes later, he returned with a small sports bag in his hands.

"Look under the table!" he said gruffly.

"In there is an old .45 Colt Government and a Smith and Wesson in .357 Magnum.

Plus 20 bullets for the revolver and a box of .45 ACP for the Colt pistol. Okay? Is that all right with you?"

"Estupendo, amigo. I knew I could count on you!" Cortez replied.

"Good, now get out of here, but come back tonight.

You know... your brother was one of my best friends! I need to think... you understand, hombre?"

"Claro, amigo, claro!"

Pascal nodded, stood up, and shook Luca's hand in a friendly farewell. Then he left the run-down bistro.

Jolanda was still waiting outside. She looked down at the ground in shame as Pascal walked past her.

He actually wanted to say something nice to the young woman at that moment, but Pascal held back. So he left it at a quick "Adéu!"

The thief with the dark blue bag swung himself onto the old Vespa, started it, and roared off.

At the same time, Jean was at the Falgas family villa. The appraiser was enjoying the magnificent view. Through the huge glass windows, you could see the entire Bay of Roses.

Mercedes had disappeared for a moment but now returned with coffee and fresh croissants.

"Well, Jean, do you like the view?"

"Oh yes, Mercedes. Your house, the huge pool and everything around it. The whole estate is simply fantastic!"

"Yes," replied the Spanish woman briefly. 'Shall we stay in here ... or would you prefer to sit outside by the pool?' Señora Falgas stood there looking a little indecisive, but extremely photogenic with the large tray in her hands. 'It would be nice to have coffee outside... in this wonderful weather,' he replied. She smiled and was overtaken by Jean, who gallantly opened the door for her.

"Gracias, Señor Jean. You are a true gentleman!" She laughed in her inimitable way.

"Si Señora, I hear that all the time," joked Sarre. The appraiser followed her, admiring the view once again.

A short time later, the two were sitting at a cozy table right by the pool, drinking coffee, eating fresh pasta, and talking. Or rather ... flirting!

Jean didn't recognize himself. Last night he had spent with Elena, but now he was on the verge of "falling in love" with the construction magnate's wife. But his feelings had betrayed him. The disappointment hurt. How could he have believed that a woman like her would be interested in a man like him? Nevertheless, he was about to repeat the same mistake, only to fall into a deep, black hole emotionally. But it felt so good to catch fire! He gave himself over to the situation.

Jean tried to savor every millisecond in the presence of the fiery Spanish woman.

They talked long and hard. Then, at some point during the conversation, Sarre got to the point.

The large, fawn-brown eyes that had been looking at him so warmly and devotedly all this time darkened. They suddenly lost their sparkle.

Her cheerful face changed and was instantly shrouded in deep sadness.

Jean couldn't help thinking of Venetian masks, which expressed absolute joy but also deepest sorrow in a black-and-white mentality.

"Oye Mercedes... Listen! You want the bloody carnage up there in the mountains to finally come to an end, don't you?" Jean reached across the table and took her hand.

"I beg you. Help me!"

Mercedes began to sob. "Why is this happening? Why?" Jean Sarre was about to say a few comforting words, but she stood up with tears in her eyes and cried to him.

"You won't be able to enjoy your heroic deed, Jean! You can't expect any help from the law. They'll probably hunt you down. It's best to disappear and forget about it! Oye Jean ... do you understand me ... before something bad happens to you too! I like you ... very much, I would ... Comprende, Señor!"

Jean sighed as Mercedes touched him tenderly on the shoulder. Once again, he felt as if everything was spinning, and he embraced the petite beauty. What's happening to me, he thought just a moment later. She kissed him and he was completely beside himself.

Perhaps the cause of his mental state was just the full moon, as silly as that sounded.

"The moon controls the tides—that much is certain! The celestial body pulls the water toward it, and me and all the other waterheads with it!" mused the completely confused Sarre.

"I like you, and I'll help you, Jean! But now let's go swimming. It'll take our minds off things!"

Jean didn't quite understand when the Spanish woman broke free and giggled as she pushed him toward the swimming pool. With a strength he would never have credited the fragile woman with, she now braced herself against his upper body until he lost his balance and fell in.

Then the slender beauty jumped in after him with a flawless dive.

The water was simply fantastic and the two splashed around like two carefree children. Slowly, their wet clothes began to annoy them. Jean was amazed by Mercedes' skillful underwater strip. She beamed at him and swung her wet bra over her head like a professional Texan lasso thrower.

Jean also stripped off his onerous clothes, except for his underwear. Then he swam to the edge of the pool to take them off.

Meanwhile, Mercedes swung herself onto a large sunbathing raft anchored in the middle of the pool. Skilfully, the beauty, wearing only a thong, pushed herself out of the water. She waved to Jean, who was busy wringing out his wet clothes.

"Hey Jean, come on! Do me a favor and rub some sunscreen on my back!"

As Sarre swam toward his hostess, he thought that this outdoor pool would be a great place for the local swimming club to hold competitions. The wooden raft that was now directly in front of him would probably have filled half of his own pool.

Unlike Señora Falgas, he didn't push himself out of the water. He unsportingly used the small ladder to climb onto the dark brown planks.

"I've been waiting here for hours for you and I'm almost burning up," she joked, turning onto her stomach and holding out a large bottle of sunscreen.

As he spread the waterproof cream on her narrow back, he tried to be as gentle as possible. However, he rubbed most of it between her narrow shoulders and tried desperately to avoid the area around her lower spine.

"You really are a gentleman, Jean! But you can rub a little harder. I'm not made of glass, after all, and I'll return the favor in a minute. You'll see!"

Jean complied, and the cautious rubbing slowly turned into a sensual massage, which quickly led to a few sensual sounds from the fiery Spaniard.

This action by the woman lying beneath him inevitably elicited a reaction from Jean, which he hoped she would not notice.

But she did, and looked demonstratively in that direction.

"Hey, Chico!" Jean Sarre blushed slightly and instinctively wanted to avoid her provocative gaze, but the black-haired woman stood up elegantly without taking her eyes off him. "Hey, it's not a big deal. It's kind of cute, actually! At least now I know you're not necessarily into guys!"

Hahaha ... don't blush ... hahaha."

Jean was speechless. He probably looked like a pubescent teenager who had been caught masturbating behind the kitchen door for the first time.

"Now lie down on your stomach, Jean. I'm going to rub cream on your broad back. But be careful that nothing gets caught between the wooden planks—how should I put it—...caught! ... Understood?"

Mercedes giggled. Jean couldn't help but laugh out loud too. Everything was so simple! He was lying on the sun lounger and letting a beautiful stranger rub his back.

Somehow the scene seemed so unreal, almost dreamlike, but he enjoyed every touch, even the most tentative ones.

Suddenly, he felt hot lips, wet hair, fiery caresses, and a body pressing wildly against him. Jean turned slowly but demonstratively so that Mercedes could find a new position. After all, it would certainly have been rather awkward to let the lively Spanish woman fall onto the hard teak planks.

Afterward, they lay, knelt, or stood. They made love, they moaned, they both breathed heavily! Jean had found a playmate in Mercedes who gave the impression of having lived a completely abstinent life for quite some time. She seemed completely uninhibited and starved.

Jean couldn't help thinking about the clip he had made. In his mind, he saw himself in a heart-shaped bed.

Sarre had been just about to come, but now Mercedes wanted to go swimming. What a shame.

"Come on, Jean! Follow me over there to the shallow end!"

Jean followed and they both swam in the nude about twenty meters to the side of the pool.

There was a raised area under the water, which was probably meant to represent a sandbank. Mercedes now wanted to make love to him in the water.

It was actually a first for the man in his late forties. When Jean entered her underwater, the feeling was so different from a few minutes earlier. Her vagina now felt cool and rough, but then, absurdly, smooth and warm again. For Jean, it was a new and yet so stimulating sensation. It felt as if there was suddenly a third force at work. Yes, exactly, it wasn't just Mercedes caressing his body. The water washed around and caressed them both. It was her assistant ... her assistant in lovemaking.

The scruffy doctor sat in front of his computer, panting loudly, and suddenly had a sense of foreboding in his stomach. To save electricity, only a small reading lamp was on, barely illuminating his desk. Slowly, he heaved his body out of his office chair and into the darkness of his study.
"Hello, is anyone there?" Eugenio Kremer whispered uncertainly into the darkness.
His heart almost jumped out of his mouth when he heard an annoyed groan.
He tried to find the light switch for the ceiling light, stumbling tremulously through the unlit room.
Had his imagination played tricks on him? The only sound he could hear at that moment was the fan of his desktop computer.
But then someone turned on the light. Now the doctor really felt like he was standing in the dark.
"Why so nervous, Eugenio? You'd almost think you had a guilty conscience!
Why, with all the good you've done... or is there something you're hiding?"
When Kremer turned around, he saw her standing there. She was holding a gun.
"What are you doing here? You should be doing your job!"
The doctor looked puzzled and rubbed his small beady eyes under his thick horn-rimmed glasses.

"You know very well, Doc, that I'm still the one who decides when and where I carry out a murder!"

"So the pain in the ass is still alive? You probably don't have my money with you either. What am I supposed to think? And what's that gun in your hand? You're disappointing me, Elena! Damn it... even though I take care of your little daughter like a father!"

Elena didn't let the obese man's accusations unsettle her. The contract killer kept the pistol in her right hand. However, she now pointed the barrel at the floor.

"What are you really doing up here?"

Eugenio's eyes twitched because he knew that his counterpart now wanted to know more about his "work" at the hospital.

"Listen, Elena!" The doctor tried to force a smile. 'You kill for money and I heal terminally ill people! That's the difference between us!"

Elena was slowly losing her temper. 'You've got to be kidding me," she replied loudly.

"You exploit poor illegals here. Damn it. You cut them open, rip out their organs to transplant them into some rich bastards. Yes, maybe you heal them. But only after you've finished off some poor bastards.

And then there's your so-called pain research! You're as humane as a damn concentration camp doctor. You're a brutal pig, Eugenio. Monsters like you aren't worth a damn!"

Now Elena had the gun pointed at him again. A fact that the doctor didn't even realize. His brain was too busy trying to figure out how his acquaintance had discovered his secret.

But suddenly he heard a bang, or rather a dull thud. At that moment, he assumed that he was finally finished. But then he looked at Elena. She slowly knelt down in front of him and fell flat on the hard linoleum floor.

"Thank you, I owe you once again, my dear!"

After Jean got back home, his thoughts turned once again to Arthos and the threat. He wasn't going to disappear, because they had taken a good friend from him. He would make the cowardly perpetrators pay for what they had done. Sarre wasn't a fearless hero, but he had an incorruptible sense of justice and nothing left to lose. Not anymore.

He had told Pascal that Señora Falgas would open the door for them, but nothing more. Now the two comrades sat together at the dining table smoking.

The Colt pistol and the heavy revolver lay in front of them.

The coffee had just finished filtering. Jean filled two cups to the brim. Except for a brief "Gracias," there was silence.

The hot, black liquid the two men were drinking was supposed to work like a magic potion. Silence, coffee, cigarettes—all of it was supposed to strengthen their senses against the hardships that awaited them—inevitably!

Then the doorbell rang. Pascal flinched. But Jean motioned to the small-time crook to stay calm by holding his index finger briefly in front of his mouth. Then he whispered.

"Psssst... Pascal! Hide in the bedroom and I don't want to hear a peep from you! Okay?"

"Okay, amigo... Are you expecting someone?"

"No! I have absolutely no idea who it is. Go on, now, but keep quiet!"

Pascal took the guns and quietly disappeared into the bedroom. Jean slowly walked to the front door and opened it.

"Hola, compagnero! How are you after that crappy night? I didn't want to bother you yesterday, but today..."

The inspector stood in the doorway and didn't look particularly happy.

Jean tried to smile, but it was tinged with sadness.

"First of all, thank you, Inspector, for having your men drive me home the night before last."

"No problem, it was no trouble at all, amigo. Once again, I'm really sorry about your dog and your SUV. I never would have believed something like that could happen!"

"Thank you, Señor Ruiz. Who could have predicted that? You read the note the boy gave me. Those people just want to scare me. They'll stop at nothing to do it."

The inspector looked at Jean skeptically. He would have given anything to be able to read the expert's thoughts.

Carlos Ruiz asked Jean who he had told about this. Jean Sarre responded by lying through his teeth.

"I don't understand, Señor Sarre!" The inspector shook his head vigorously. "The person or persons who taught you this lesson think differently!"

"They know you have something and could go public with it. If you had just one copy of those videos, I'd at least have something to work with ... if only I had ..."

Jean shrugged his shoulders in shame.

"Listen, Jean! I'll keep asking around. Then I'll apply for a search warrant for the hospital.

But it's too dangerous for you here. We're currently at a standstill with the case of your blown-up car. It's best if you leave Catalonia, at least until we catch the perpetrators. Do you understand?" I've already booked you a flight because my boss wants you out of the line of fire. He insists that you take it!"

Jean was completely baffled. He definitely hadn't expected that. He was more or less being expelled from the country.

"You can forget it, Police Inspector! I've rented this house for a long time. Besides, I wouldn't quit my job at Estrella Insurance."

"That's final, my friend. Everything has already been arranged! My boss has taken care of everything. Your employer has also been informed. There is no alternative. Unless you prefer protective custody! Don't be stupid, partner. Take your quarter of a million and get out of here!"

Jean stood rooted to the spot. Silently, he watched as the inspector took a ticket out of his jacket pocket. Without a word, he took it without even looking at it.

"Don't you even care where you're flying to tomorrow morning?"

Jean shook his head. Almost defiantly, he pressed his lips together.

"No!"

"Well... my superior has arranged everything to your satisfaction, señor!"

"Damn it, who the hell is your superior, inspector?"

"His name is Rodriguez," replied the police officer. "Our district attorney, Franco Rodriguez. A nice man, believe me, Jean!"

CHAPTER 10: *Fuerteventura*

From above, the island looked like a lunar landscape. Jean couldn't help thinking of Napoleon Bonaparte. His enemies had also sent him into exile. First to the beautiful island of Elba, then ... after the Waterloo disaster, finally to Saint Helena. He too felt like he was being sent into exile. Admittedly, there was more here than goats, but the view from the airplane window did not bode well. High waves, little greenery, and an extreme amount of sand. Welcome to the island.
Welcome to Fuerteventura!
After checking out of the island airport in Puerto del Rosario with a few package tourists, he took a completely battered taxi north. They had rented a small apartment for him here in Corralejo. He could only guess who. Either the public prosecutor's office or his employer. He pondered this briefly. There were more important things to think about.
He had to get back. As quickly as possible. Of course, he couldn't show up as Jean Sarre.

He paid the taxi, wondered why the apartment key fit, threw his suitcase on the bed, grabbed his cell phone, and dialed a number.

On the small nightstand, Jean noticed a large bronze figure that he found extremely ugly. Somehow a mixture of an Oscar statue and a Dali artwork, he guessed.

"Hola!" At first, no one answered. But then the appraiser heard restrained laughter.

"Ey amigo, I thought I'd have to clean up this mess by myself!"

"You, or rather you, are a joker, Pascal! I just got here. I haven't even unpacked my things yet!"

"Then don't bother, hombre! You can be back here by tomorrow at the latest.

Your new ID is already in the works and my friend Luca is taking care of it. Is your address still the same?"

After giving the Spanish petty crook his current address again, Jean ended the conversation. Completely exhausted, he collapsed onto the bed.

Then, sometime during the night, his smartphone rang.

Jean jumped up. At first, he didn't even know where he was. In the dark room, he had no sense of direction, and only the flashing display periodically illuminated the room with a bluish light.

"Sarre," he answered, agitated.

At first, the connection was poor. But then he recognized Pascal's frantic voice.

"Hey Sarre... you... moo... um... out!" "What... what... I don't understand you... the connection is bad!"

Jean got up and shuffled across the bedroom, still fully clothed and completely drenched in sweat. He kept hoping that he would eventually understand Pascal. But then the connection was cut off.

He immediately dialed the cell phone he had given Pascal several times. On the fourth try, he finally answered.

"Jean, can you hear me ... listen to me carefully!"

Meanwhile, Jean heard a faint creaking sound that seemed to be coming from the front door.

"What's going on, Pascal? Fuck, I think someone's trying to break in!"

"Mierda ... Jean. Luca called me earlier. A hitman has been sent after you ... his name is Auguste, or something like that. From what I hear, he likes to play with knives. Try to get out of there, hombre!"

"Your warning comes a little late, Pascal!"

Jean hung up and turned off his cell phone. He carefully placed it under the bedspread. Now he could hear the wooden floor creaking in front of the bedroom door.

Jean threw his suitcase on the bed. He quickly threw the bedspread over it.

He had to defend himself against this killer named Auguste somehow. A knife-wielding man, well, that improved his chances, of course.

In the dark room, he suddenly remembered the pretty-ugly statue. He fumbled around a few times before finally getting his hands on it.

Then the bedroom door opened almost silently from the outside.

A figure dressed in black entered the room on tiptoe. Slowly but surely, she moved purposefully toward Jean's bed.

Auguste preferred to use his old Cold Steel knife with the kraton handle. It was handy, razor sharp, and easy to clean. It had already served him well on several missions. Silent killing had become something of a passion for him.

Eventually, his time in the Foreign Legion came to an end. At least he was given a new identity when he left the service, but he disliked his new name from the start.

"Auguste Moinet" sounded like impoverished nobility to his ears.

Unlike him, his superior had at least had a say in his new name.

It had annoyed him so much at the time that he could still remember the man well. "Sarre ... Jean Sarre!"

Auguste stabbed him. Once, twice... Then, when he realized he was attacking an old suitcase, the hitman felt a damn hard blow to his head. He lost consciousness.

Some time later, Auguste was rudely awakened. Jean had tied him up with cable ties and thrown him in front of the bed.

"Well, well, well, it's you again! The world is a damn small place, isn't it?"

"Every legionnaire is a brother! Have you forgotten that, Auguste? How long do you think we fought together under the tricolor? We sang 'Westerwald' and 'Lily Marleen' together ...

Do you remember how I trained you? Besides, I saved your shitty ass several times. Now you want to stab me like a pig to thank me?

But I knew it even back then! You damned asshole! I knew even then that our code of honor meant nothing to you! Back in Africa, you would have shot that little boy without a second thought. If Henry hadn't stopped you first!"

Auguste didn't say anything at first. How he would have loved to wipe the blood from his face, but his hands were tied behind his back.

"Who sent you, Auguste? Tell me who sent you and I'll let you go!"

Auguste grinned inwardly. Full of malice, he began to speak.

"A misunderstanding ... if I had known it was you! I had no idea ... brother!

Please untie me and then we'll talk! I swear!"

Jean went over to him. Hesitantly, he took the combat knife to cut through the cable ties. Auguste groaned, stretched, and shook his arms to get his blood circulation going again.

"Thanks, chief," he said. The former legionnaire flashed his broadest smile.

Auguste slowly sat up, turned away from Jean, and frantically massaged his wrists.

The next moment, he abruptly turned toward his former instructor. He attempted to surprise him with a "sidekick" to the lower abdomen. But Jean Sarre was alert.

He caught Auguste's leg with his left hand. He held it tight, then struck with his right.

The former soldier's nose broke like glass. Shortly afterwards, fresh blood mixed with the dried secretions from the head wound.

"You bastard!" groaned the hitman. Suddenly, he grabbed the knife Jean had thrown onto the bed.

"Now it's your turn!" Jean backed away and Auguste stared at his opponent with hatred.

"Who sent you, Auguste?" Jean repeated his question, without taking his eyes off the long knife the killer was shifting from hand to hand.

"Someone from Catalonia, you cocksucker. Take a guess! Someone is paying me a lot of money to send you to the happy hunting grounds! You really pissed someone off! Now let me do my job and just die!"

Auguste jumped forward, trying to ram the knife into Jean's throat. But the stab missed and Sarre countered with lightning speed.

He kicked his opponent in the groin and simultaneously struck him on both ears with the palms of his hands, so hard that his eardrums burst.

The hitman dropped to his knees, fell like a sack of potatoes, and unfortunately fell onto his own knife.

Jean had already heard the sound once or twice before. A short, unspectacular "flap" when a blade pierces the chest.

But there was still time. Sarre repeated his question, relatively emotionless.

"Who sent you, Auguste? Now tell me! If you talk, I'll get you to the nearest hospital as fast as I can!"

But Auguste didn't hear him. The only thing the hitman could hear was a whistling sound.

A squeaking and whistling that grew louder. The sound came from his lungs, which were collapsing. Then Auguste choked on his own blood.

Jean sat down on the bed. His gaze fell on the battered suitcase. Sure, he had often argued with Auguste back then, but was that the reason, or just a stupid coincidence?

The killer must have known that he was supposed to kill his former instructor. Or maybe not?

But it didn't matter. Auguste was dead, lying about two meters in front of Jean's feet in a pool of his own blood. The expert, who had just lit a cigarette, inhaled the smoke deeply, indulged briefly in memories, took his smartphone and turned it back on. Then he pressed the redial option.

After a short, loud, hectic but thank God reassuring conversation with Pascal, Sarre let himself fall lengthwise onto the bed. All he could do now was wait.

Pascal would talk to his acquaintance. Hopefully, this mysterious acquaintance would hire someone to clean up Jean's room by tomorrow morning at the latest.

After all, the body had to disappear from Fuerteventura. He needed help!

Two hours later, there was a knock at the door. Jean woke up with a start. He cautiously opened the door. Standing outside was a small, thin little guy grinning from ear to ear.

"Buenas Noches, Señor. I'm here to sort something out for you. Here I am!"

Jean sighed with relief. He actually wanted to say something to the little man in the black suit. But he simply wriggled past him and into the apartment.

"Just call me Gonzalez, Señor." The man reminded Jean of an attack force.

"Now show me the job. Quickly! Understood? We don't have much time. You have to help—okay, okay, okay? Where... where... is it? Ah, there it is!" His voice was almost breaking.

"A lively, hectic, unpleasant dwarf," thought Jean.

"Buen... good, señor!" The man who called himself Gonzalez slowly calmed down. 'Well... good?' The former legionnaire was immediately interrupted again.

"Calm down, now calm down! I have to think!"

Jean was slowly beginning to get annoyed with his helper.

"Listen,... I..."

"Calm down, okay señor!"

"Hombre, you need to find a bunch of cleaning rags and cleaning supplies right now. And a bucket of hot water. The floor needs to be scrubbed until it shines. I'm going to be gone for a moment. When I come back, the three of us are going for a drive!"

"But?"... Once again, Jean was rudely interrupted. Then the little whirlwind disappeared as quickly as he had come.

Far, far away, somewhere in the Pyrenees, a blonde woman with a disability had a completely different problem. When Elena came to, she thought her head was going to explode, or at least that it would do so any second.

The throbbing, the hellish pain...

Elena lay alone on a bench, trying to reach her head with her hands. But it just didn't work. Getting up was out of the question, because she was completely immobilized. No wonder, because Nurse Rita had taken great care to restrain her.

It took Elena a few minutes to realize her predicament. Why had she let herself be taken by surprise like that? For a moment, she no longer felt the uncontrollable headache. Instead, the blonde woman was annoyed at her own unprofessional behavior.

She should have liquidated the fat bastard without any preliminaries, but after all, there was still her daughter Katharina.

"Damn it," she thought, 'just pull the trigger and then get Katharina out of here.' But she could forget that now. Elena was realistic enough to know that Dr. Eugenio Kremer would not spare her now.

Tied up by her arms and legs, lying on the hard bench, something happened to her that hadn't happened in decades. She began to sob.

Her tears ran down her temples, mixing with the congealed blood from her head injury.

She cried quietly because her Katharina was probably only a few meters away, just a few blankets above her. Maybe the little girl was playing with one of her dolls and had no idea what was happening. She hadn't even been able to say goodbye to her Kathi. How she would have loved to hold her daughter in her arms one last time.

About sixty-five feet above his desperate prisoner, Dr. Eugenio Kremer sat in his office. He stared at his cell phone with relief.

The text message that had just arrived lifted his spirits considerably.

"That little problem has been taken care of," he thought aloud, his thick lips curving into a broad grin. He took his black horn-rimmed glasses off his nose to clean the thick lenses with a paper tissue.

Suddenly, the phone rang. The doctor was so startled that he almost dropped his glasses.

"Hospital Pedro Leon…"

"Hola Señor Kremer, que tal?"

Eugenio had to swallow.

"Bien y tu?"

The person on the other end of the line could ruin all his efforts. Eugenio knew that, of course.

On the other hand, he was fed up with kowtowing, but for now he had to obey.

"Yes … when can I expect you? … Yes … yes …"

Eugenio began to sweat. After hanging up, he pressed his beeper.

He had to talk to Rita and let her in on his plans once again. What would he do without her?

Eugenio Kremer sat in his executive chair and ran his fingers through his hair. Finally, there was a knock and the head nurse entered the room, which was bathed in gloomy artificial light.

For the next twenty minutes, the two of them discussed what to do next. They debated and argued. Whenever Eugenio reacted almost hysterically, Rita was able to calm him down again.

"Don't drive yourself crazy, Eugenio! Together we can do this. Don't worry! I'll prepare everything."

"I'm counting on you, Rita. The last few days… Everything has to go on as before. You have to promise me!"

"Claro, jefe! Now make yourself comfortable and lean back, doctor!"

Rita leaned over her boss. Once again, she managed to relax him after a short time.

"Oh… my goddess," he groaned. Then, more or less kindly, he handed Rita the tissue he had just used to clean his glasses.

At about the same time, two men drove out to sea in the moonlight. On the small fishing boat, Gonzalez set about preparing everything necessary. He never tired of giving Jean more tasks to do.

"So, we're almost ready, Señor Sarre! I'm really proud of you, hombre!" In the moonlight, the little man's broad grin looked almost diabolical. Jean had already stopped cursing under his breath. It was damn hard work getting the naked corpse into a neoprene suit. But finally, the dead man looked like what he was supposed to be. Gonzalez stopped the engine a short time later and lowered a used surfboard into the water. Then the men threw the dead hitman overboard together.

"It'll look like he had an accident while surfing." Gonzalez patted Jean on the shoulder in a friendly manner. "The current will carry him far south. Even if he's found sooner, the fish will have cleaned up all the traces. Remember that the next time you order seafood!" He laughed loudly, then held out a chrome hip flask to Jean.

Jean hesitated, which made Gonzalez laugh hoarsely.

"Come on, hombre, take it, it'll warm you up! The cognac isn't poisoned, I swear!"

Jean had to grin too and took a long sip.

Gonzalez was right! The alcohol felt good! After a night like that!

The fishing boat rocked from side to side as the men headed back.

Gonzalez had already burned the killer's clothes. Nothing would point to the nighttime attack. At least, that was the hope!

Once ashore, the two men conferred briefly after Gonzalez had slipped the German a fake passport and a plane ticket.

"My client has already taken care of the financial arrangements. He wishes you a safe journey back to Catalonia. Adiós y Buen Viaje!"

Jean wanted to thank the little man, but darkness had already swallowed him up again.

Meanwhile, the mood at the Falgas household was gloomy. Mercedes was once again annoyed with her Juanito. The head of the construction company had come home from a business meeting just an hour ago, much too late for the dinner she had prepared.

Juan Falgas sat down without saying a word, took a bite, chewed, and promptly spat the piece of meat onto his porcelain plate in disgust.

"This food is fucking cold! Our cook's on vacation and you're already trying to poison me!"

Mercedes sat at the other end of the table and didn't say a word.

She didn't show any emotion. She no longer wanted to appease her husband with submissive excuses.

Actually, she was surprised at herself. For a moment, she felt like she was about to explode, but nothing happened.

Not a flash of anger, not even the slightest sob. Somehow, Mercedes felt nothing but complete emptiness. Then the Spanish woman began to smile. Yes, she just smiled.

This "Mona Lisa" smile completely threw her husband off balance.

If she had cried, Juan would have had a field day rubbing salt into the wound.

If she had cried, made herself small in front of him, he would have accused her again of being a complete failure. But she was beaming at him. So he downed his wine in one go and jumped up. He had to leave the room immediately. He wanted to go outside, feeling that everything was suffocating him here.

But as he stood in the doorway, he turned back to his wife.

"I ..." He broke off. "You do remember that we have an appointment in Vidasacra tomorrow morning, don't you?

We're leaving at seven sharp tomorrow morning! Right on the dot! Understood?"

I'm going to bed now. Okay ... I'm exhausted. See you tomorrow morning."

"See you tomorrow," she replied quietly. Now that her husband had left the dining room, her decision was set in stone. Final!

As dawn broke, Pascal and Luca stood in front of the airport building in Girona.

"I still can't believe it."

"What?" asked Pascal meekly.

"What do you think? That you dragged me into your mess after all, Tonto!"

Pascal knew that it would be wise not to respond.

He quickly tried to change the subject.

"Hombre, just look at all these rental cars standing around here completely unattended!"

Luca was boiling, but he would calm down quickly.

He knew his dead brother Fernando's best friend that well.

"Gonzo called me from Fuerteventura.

Everything went well, but now the little bastard wants his money, claro!

I hope your French friend pays me this morning, amigo.

I already had to front it! That's the only reason I'm here. Got it?

If not... I'll break every rib in his body and yours..."

Luca hesitated briefly, but didn't finish the threat. Instead, he put on his wolfish "Jack Nicholson grin" again. His companion got goose bumps when the gray-haired giant pinched his cheek in a friendly manner.

"And you, my dear Pascal, afterwards... your jaw, claro? Hahaha..."

CHAPTER 11: *Back in Catalonia*

Exhausted, excited, with a new identity but ready for anything, Jean Sarre set foot on Spanish soil again. Everything went smoothly at customs, and when he left the airport building in Girona, he felt like he had been transported back in time.

Back then, he had nothing to lose either. He didn't care about his own life, or how long it would last.

There were times when all that mattered was the thrill. Only when enough adrenaline was pumping through his veins did he feel truly alive.

A few years ago, he forced himself to change his ways so he could lead a normal life.

His punishment had been paid. During his time in the Legion, he had certainly used up dozens of guardian angels.

Now the expert stood there in jeans and a black T-shirt, a light jacket thrown over his shoulder.

Jean searched the crowd for a familiar face while talking on the phone. At the same time, the former legionnaire desperately rummaged for his cigarettes when he saw Pascal waving wildly at him.

The two greeted each other briefly, patted each other on the shoulder, before walking over to a black Audi A8, in front of which the bartender Luca was waiting grumpily.

"Hola, ... here comes our friend. Bienvenido! Welcome back to the Costa Brava! Did you have a good flight? I hope so! And I hope, especially for you, that you'll pay me what you owe me today!"

Jean paused briefly, looking the dangerous-looking man straight in the eye. Then he wanted to shake his hand.

But Luca kept his arms planted on his hips. Instead, he returned Jean's gaze with a grim poker face.

Pascal opened the tailgate of the large Audi for Jean. He motioned wordlessly to Sarre to stow his luggage inside.

Now Jean had to smile. After placing the small suitcase in the huge trunk, he turned back to Luca to respond to the unfriendly giant.

"Don't worry, hombre! Just drive me to Empuriabrava. You'll get your money there!"

Luca hesitated briefly, glanced at Pascal out of the corner of his eye, and at the same time exhaled audibly through his nose.

"Let's go, Señor Sarre, or whatever your name may be! Come on, let's get going! By the way, I'm getting ten thousand euros for the advance payment from Señor Gonzalez. Another ten thousand for the fake papers! Just so you know, Señor!"

"No problem!" Jean replied briefly. Then they drove off with screeching tires and quickly left the Girona airport area behind them.

After about an hour and a half, the unlikely trio arrived in Empuriabrava. However, before they reached their destination, there was an interlude, or rather a serious disagreement, between Jean and Luca on the outskirts of a small village.

The reason was a small black dog that Luca almost ran over due to his reckless driving.

Jean, who was sitting next to Luca in the passenger seat, saw the dog run onto the road. When he saw that Luca wasn't reacting, he grabbed the steering wheel of the A8.

"Watch out, Luca, be careful! Man, brake!"

"Pendejo, tonto... Idiot, what are you doing? Damn asshole!"

The Audi swerved and spun around its own axis. The car ended up sideways on the dusty road.

"I should knock your teeth out right now. Damn... what a... if you didn't owe me twenty thousand!"

Now Jean showed no reaction, and Pascal was silent, sweating in the back seat.

Luca had a strong urge to break all his passenger's bones, but he had other things on his mind. So he drove the car into a small side street to avoid attracting attention. Then he got out and walked several meters away, still talking excitedly and frantically on the phone.

The small, shaggy schnauzer mix was still sitting on the side of the road. The stray scratched nervously behind his ear.

Luca spotted him, ended his phone call, and when the animal still made no move to leave, the giant walked quickly toward the dog. He kicked the schnauzer loudly, cursing. The poor little guy tried desperately to get away, whimpering loudly.

Now Jean reacted. It was extremely rare, but there were situations in which he could totally lose it. This was one of them!

When he saw Luca kicking the black dog in the rearview mirror, he somehow associated the scene with Arthos. He immediately thought of his Doberman, who had been killed deliberately, slid into the driver's seat, started the car, and drove backwards toward Luca.

The giant stared at the white taillights in confusion for a moment, then yanked open the driver's door of the Audi A8.

He grabbed Jean by the throat, but when he tried to pull the expert out of the car, he misjudged his strength a little.

Jean quickly freed himself from Luca's grip. At the same time, he punched the six-foot-tall Spaniard hard in the nose. Luca literally exploded when he tasted his own blood. He then punched the air wildly several times. Now he also took a kick in the stomach and a right jab from Jean Sarre.

"That's a down payment on your twenty thousand," he remarked dryly.

After being hit abruptly on the tip of his chin, Luca collapsed. He fell to his knees in slow motion, then kissed the Catalan street dust headfirst.

The knocked-out Luca reminded Pascal, who was still sitting in the back seat and couldn't get over his amazement, of a felled tree.

"Come on, Pascal, get out of the car! Help me!
We have to put your friend, that idiot, in the trunk. We can't just leave him lying here."

Pascal obeyed reverently, shaking his head. After stowing all the junk they could find in the car, the two of them used all their strength to heave the tall pimp into the spacious trunk.

"That was crazy, Jean. I never would have believed you could knock him out so easily. Respect, hombre... I can't believe it, but shouldn't we at least take Luca to a doctor or a hospital nearby?"

Jean shook his head and looked at him pityingly.

"How naive are you? We can't trust anyone anymore. Not this guy, not in a million years! It's easy to predict what your big friend would do first. He'd either call the cops or those dirty bastards up in the mountains, for cash, of course!"

Pascal just shrugged his shoulders and furrowed his brow. Then he got back into the Audi. This time, however, he took the passenger seat and reached into the glove compartment to take out a chrome hip flask.

"One sip and no more. Comprende?"

"Muy bien, amigo," Pascal replied quietly. After Jean had also taken a small sip of the brandy, a slight smile returned to his face.

On the drive to Empuriabrava, Jean explained to his passenger that they would have to change their plans. Pascal listened.

He would have loved to take another sip from the flask, but he had to agree with Jean.

After all, they had to remain in control of their senses, because soon he would be facing either his brother's murderer or his God.

The man in the white Ford Mustang couldn't help but grin.

If anyone could see him now, he would most likely have left a lasting impression.

Because then they would have seen mostly snow-white teeth.

The black man, dressed all in black and sitting in his V8, had his eyes on the driveway.

He continued to be amused by a man who was going about his work in an almost amateurish manner. The guy was wearing blue, dirty overalls that were two sizes too small. Of course, it could also be that his belly fat simply no longer fit into the coarse fabric.

It happened as it had to happen. When he bent down again to pry open the front door, the seam of his pants burst. The worker became so enraged that he kicked the door frame, injuring his right foot in the process. He then hopped around on his left leg, cursing, and lost a small revolver, which landed on the stone floor. By now, it was almost slapstick for the spectators. The man in the car had to cover his mouth with his hand to keep from laughing out loud or even biting his tongue.

After much back and forth, the door finally opened. The clumsy unlucky fellow limped into the apartment. Inside, it looked terrible. Everything was in disarray. The cupboards had been knocked over. Everything was scattered across the floor. The man made some space for himself on a leather couch, maneuvered his rear end onto it, and briefly raised his battered leg. Then he began to leisurely search his pockets. His face turned red when he realized that he must have lost his gun somewhere.

Louis Sanchez thought frantically. He tried to speed things up by repeatedly hitting his forehead with his right hand while tearing at his black, curly hair with his left. At that moment, he felt completely overwhelmed. Then he remembered that he had volunteered for this job. Yes, he had practically imposed himself on it.

He, the small, plump Spaniard with black curls, who not only looked like a comedian but also often behaved like one. Somehow, he resembled the French actor, comedian, and author 'Coluche', who sadly passed away too soon. Louis liked to think of himself as a tough guy. So he tried everything he could to be seen as one.

In doing so, he kept putting his foot in his mouth, especially with his acquaintances.

He was a not exactly gigantic, flippant layabout who had learned nothing. So he found it difficult to hold down a regular job. No, Louis had to get by as a petty crook, much like the Cortez brothers.

But then, some time ago, he had knocked down a dangerous pimp during a fight.

After that, he was on the verge of having business cards printed with the words:

"Louis Sanchez—Martial Arts Expert—Hand Edge and Boxing Champion Killer!"

Every evening in his local bar, he would let everyone know what a dangerous guy he was. It didn't matter whether they wanted to hear it or not.

Full of pathos, he told the same story over and over again. Woe betide anyone who showed signs of boredom.

He would then point to the edge of his right hand and swear about its deadly effect.

Some people feigned respect, but behind his back they called him a "urinal killer."

The more Sanchez told his story, the more he believed his somewhat embellished version.

But on the evening in question, things turned out a little differently. The little Spaniard was sitting at the bar of his local pub, making fun of everything and everyone after several shots of schnapps.

At some point, a big, burly guy sat down next to him.

When sober, Louis would have instinctively held back, or at least moved several meters away, but the alcohol had removed all his inhibitions.

At some point, the bald man had had enough. Although the bartender had warned Louis several times to control himself, a fight eventually broke out.

Louis noticed that his neighbor at the bar stood up in disgust, and then he added fuel to the fire.

"By the way, I like your hairstyle. You have a head like a polished toilet bowl, amigo!"

Now the man, who used to be a kickboxing champion and now had to earn his living as a bouncer and occasional pimp, had had enough.

The baldie literally tucked Louis under his arm. Then, amid general laughter, he made his way to the restroom.

Louis didn't have the slightest chance of freeing himself from the grip. Slowly, he began to sober up again.

Gradually, it became uncomfortable for him, because the champion hadn't forgotten the toilet bowl comparison. He was just about to place Louis' head in it.

Now the little curly-headed person fought with all his might. He kicked around, tried to brace himself with his hands and feet, but to no avail. Again, his head was forced under the water. The flush was also activated.

Louis now had the feeling that his last hour had come. Unfortunately, he also knew that he was to blame.

Suddenly, the hand on his head opened and the pressure eased. Louis gasped for air and held on to the toilet bowl with both hands.

Eventually, after several minutes, he turned around and saw his adversary lying on the floor, cramped and dead as a doornail.

The man had had a heart attack from the excitement.

Louis embellished the story slightly in his favor, however.

When he told it, he said that he had sent the bald giant to the afterlife with a professional karate chop.

Of course, after warning his enemy several times about his martial arts skills. But when the bald man pulled out a weapon, he had to defend himself, didn't he? The giant didn't give him a choice!

Yes, unless you're tired of living, it's better not to mess with "Louis the Killer Sanchez."

Now, as "Killer Louis" frantically tried to remember where he could have lost his revolver, he tried just as frantically to encourage himself.

Outside, yes, outside the house, he still had his old Smith & Wesson, but where was it now? Louis groaned in annoyance, stood up, and limped back toward the front door.

When he opened the door to heave his body outside, he saw the revolver lying on the ground in front of him.

At the same time, a man of African descent was also making his way toward him, unnoticed by the curly-haired man.

"Hey, hombre, we know each other!" the black man said with a laugh. Louis was startled, hesitated briefly, picked up the gun, and almost wet his torn pants.

"Get out of here, gegege ... get out of here!"

Louis stammered with excitement. At the same time, he stared at snow-white teeth.

Now the black man started laughing at him at the top of his lungs. Louis didn't like that at all. Trembling and with a bright red face, he pointed the loaded .38 Special at his opponent, who was quickly approaching him.

Suddenly and predictably, what always happened to Louis happened to him again.

The revolver's cylinder opened unexpectedly, and the six bullets fell to the ground with a clatter.

The last thing Louis saw while he was still conscious were the snow-white teeth. Then the black fist came crashing down on him.

On the way to Empuriabrava, Jean smoked one cigarette after another. He literally devoured the Lucky Strikes. Pascal, who was nervously shifting back and forth in the passenger seat, was also smoking like a chimney.

It was only when the big Audi drove past the sports airport that the two resumed their conversation.

"What are you going to do now, Jean? How should we proceed?"

Sarre replied that they had to get there first. Then he grabbed his beeping cell phone to read a text message that had just come in.

"Estupendo!" he said with a smile, and then the two of them had already reached Falconera Street.

"Stop here! We need to assess the situation first," Pascal said briefly, but Jean drove straight to number 22. As he drove through the open gate, his passenger became visibly nervous.

"Why is the gate open?" The Catalan looked somewhat irritated.

Only when the car had stopped and the steel gate closed again did Jean turn back to Pascal.

"Are you actually afraid of the dark?"

"What? ... You want to know if I'm afraid of the dark? What kind of stupid question is that?" Pascal slapped his forehead.

Jean had to laugh.

"Hahaha, no Pascal ... Hahaha ... Of the dark ... Of the bogeyman!"

"Well, ... then let yourself be surprised."

After they got out of the car, they walked toward the open front door.

Once inside, Jean was greeted by a familiar sight.

A so-called "déjà vu"! Once again, the contents of all the cabinets and drawers were scattered across the floor.

"If you'd given me more time, I would have tidied up before you arrived," said a voice from the background.

Pascal wanted to reach for his gun, but Jean put his hand on his shoulder to calm him down.

"Don't be afraid of the black man!" he whispered with a laugh.

Then Pascal saw him too. The man who was proud to be a great individual of the "people of color" suddenly stood in front of him and held out his hand. It took a moment, then Pascal shook it. The black man's mouth twisted into a slight grin that grew wider and wider.

"I've been waiting a long time for this! Besides, I knew it would happen."

Jean hugged his old friend.

"What happened, Henry?"

"That you'd need my help again someday, bro!"

Henry was triumphant, but Jean's feelings toward him were rather mixed at the moment.

The two had served together in the past. They had often had to watch each other's backs.

But in these times, the situation was somewhat different.

As a civilian, Jean was trying to maintain a healthy distance from his former comrade-in-arms. Until recently, the insurance clerk had been planning to finally live a normal life.

Henry Batiste, however, was somewhat different in this regard.

Unlike Jean, he simply could not and would not submit to social constraints. As a result, the views of the two comrades drifted far apart.

The tall, dark-skinned man with South African roots earned his living after his military service primarily as a drug and arms dealer. In the meantime, however, he had multiplied his fortune through dubious stock market deals.

As a result, he now owned several bars and sex clubs.

Under normal circumstances, Jean would have avoided contact with his former best friend. But in this situation and for this plan, Henry was simply the best man for the job. Besides, he was probably also an additional life insurance policy.

After the two former companions had greeted each other, Henry sniffed Pascal a little.

Jean took advantage of this time and went straight behind the house to check out his hiding place.

Somehow, he had a strange feeling in his stomach when he passed the gagged and bound chubby curly-haired boy sitting on a chair.

Judging by how chaotic the apartment looked, they had been there for quite some time. No one had disturbed them while they were searching.

Whoever had done this had certainly done a thorough job. The hiding place was empty.

Jean stood there in disbelief, completely speechless. The former French Foreign Legionnaire stared past the old palm tree at the natural stone wall.

Was the inspector behind this? Was half the money not enough for him?

He almost feared so! But he also knew that it would be difficult to ask Carlos Ruiz about it.

Jean knew that it was wise not to trust anyone now. Perhaps that was the real reason they had sent him to Fuerteventura. That way, they could be reasonably sure that he wouldn't take the remaining two hundred and fifty thousand with him on the plane. So they could search for it in peace.

"Well, what's going on, did you see a ghost?"

Jean flinched. He hadn't heard Pascal coming.

"So it looks like those guys were luckier than us, right?"

Jean nodded.

"You know, Jean, there's a silver lining to all this!"

Jean raised his eyebrows.

"If you don't have anything left, you don't have anything to lose. Comprende?"

"Claro cabrón?"

Jean had to smile, whether he wanted to or not.

"Claro!"

Henry also came over to the old wall. He was surprised that Pascal and Jean were in such a good mood.

"Hey, hombres, could you two jokers help me out for once? Besides, you still have that Luca in the trunk, don't you?"

The two looked at each other in confusion. That's right, Luca was still there. Jean had a few questions for him.

When the men pulled him out of the trunk again, Luca complained in every way possible.

His face was bright red. His gray braid stood out and somehow resembled a radio antenna.

"You damn bastards. I'll kill you both for this!"

Luca was boiling with rage. As soon as he was back on his feet, he immediately started attacking Jean.

But Jean's leg shot forward. The innkeeper was already getting a powerful kick in the stomach. Luca doubled over in pain while Jean twisted his right arm behind his back.

Now Jean pushed him into the house.

"Man, you haven't forgotten anything!" Henry was impressed as he took several cable ties out of his jacket.

"My dear Jean, I actually thought you'd become a real wimp by now, but look at you!"

Yes, Jean was also surprised at himself. It had been a while since his last martial arts training. But apparently, it was like riding a bike. When Henry was still his sparring partner, the two of them had broken each other's noses more than once. In the military, they often practiced close combat because, after all, you had to keep yourself fit somehow. Henry had been into kickboxing in his youth, and Jean had trained diligently in judo, Krav Maga, and taekwondo as a child.

Be that as it may, both were now approaching fifty. After the scuffle, Jean quickly realized that he was no longer the youngest. In addition, he still had pain from the motorcycle accident.

Meanwhile, two men tied to chairs with cable ties were trading insults. In the wild, the two would probably have killed each other by now. Luca insulted the little curly-haired man in the worst possible way, and he wasn't the only one.

After a brief interrogation, Jean knew what he needed to know.

The scoundrel named Louis Sanchez talked like a waterfall. His employer, Luca, shook his head in disgust.

The Spanish innkeeper had hired Sanchez at short notice to ambush Jean, rob him, and perhaps even kill him.

Luca was only interested in the money. At no point did he intend to help Pascal and Jean in any way, let alone accompany them to the mountains.

"Now listen carefully, both of you!" Sarre remarked without any visible emotion.

"You both have a choice.

Either you accompany us to Vidasacra, or I will kill you both right here on the spot. Trust me, Luca, I wouldn't have any problem doing it!"

Luca's face turned bright red again, but he didn't say a word. The giant just glared hatefully at the men standing around him, especially Jean.

Louis, who was about to wet himself out of sheer fear, began to stutter again.

"I, I, I'll go with them, but please don't kill me!"

The small, fat crook stammered with excitement.

Meanwhile, Henry grinned incessantly at Pascal. He knew very well that the Spaniard had also completely misjudged his comrade Jean.

But secretly, both he and Pascal were pleased about this, because it was the only way they would be able to survive in the mountains.

After both the petty criminal Pascal and Jean had explained the situation to the black man, Henry agreed to run a few errands. The three men then discussed how to proceed.

"Well, hombres," Jean looked at his wristwatch. "It's already 12:00 noon. Time flies!

Henry, I suggest you get us something to eat first. You're the only one who can move around outside normally at the moment."

Henry nodded briefly.

"After that," Jean remarked, "you need to work through this list."

Henry raised his eyebrows as he looked at Jean's note.

"RV, Blaser System R93 caliber 300 Winchester Magnum sniper rifle, a Lupara, plastic explosives, ... and so on and so forth. All by this afternoon. Well ... you're entertaining me, hombre!"

It wasn't the first time Jean had given instructions to his former legionnaire comrade. Henry knew that Jean's plans always made sense. At least that had been the case during their time together in the service. So he set off to buy food for the men.

In the meantime, Jean Sarre turned his attention to his prisoners. He still had some convincing to do with Luca. At about the same time that Henry arrived, loaded down with groceries in a rather tatty motorhome, Sarre was able to free the two Spaniards from their bonds. Henry walked past the men in a visibly bad mood, and when Jean asked him what had happened, he replied after a moment's hesitation.

Henry Batiste had borrowed this old Fiat camper van from an acquaintance nearby. However, he had to leave his snow-white Mustang there, of course. He wasn't happy about that at all.

"Damn it, Jean, if I pick up my car and it has even one scratch on it, I'll send you the bill! You can count on it!"

Jean just grinned, but Luca, who was still rubbing his wrists where his hands had been tied, made a relaxing remark.

"Hey, hombre, your friend just told us that there's a lot of money waiting for us in that crazy horror hospital, and even if we split the cash between the five of us, there'll be enough left for the paint job. Comprende?"

Henry scratched his head, and after the five men had fortified themselves with fresh coffee, a few baguettes, and plenty of sausage and cheese, he took Jean aside.

Henry asked Sarre if he was even aware of the two security risks, Luca and Louis, but Jean reassured him that he would keep a close eye on the two scoundrels.

Shortly after the meal, Henry set off again.

He had been on the phone with two acquaintances from the area and seemed quite pleased when he returned.

"Well, how did it go? Were you able to get everything?"

Henry said yes.

"However, I only have a normal Blaser R93 hunting rifle in 308 caliber. You should even remember the rifle. We took it hunting with us a few years ago."

Jean smiled and remembered.

Exactly ... that rifle ... About three years ago, Henry had persuaded him to go wild boar hunting in the Pyrenees.

Together with three other hunters, they spent a weekend in the mountains. They had quite a bit of luck hunting.

On the very first evening, Jean shot a small boar. Even Henry bagged a small sow. Encouraged by their hunting success and after several shots of schnapps, interrupted by loud hunting songs, the men agreed to go hunting again soon.

However, there was to be no sequel. When they returned, the expert found out that Henry was not only dealing in weapons but also in drugs.

Jean confronted his comrade loudly, but Henry showed little remorse.

On the contrary, he even offered Jean a share in his drug deals.

Jean refused in disgust and called his now former friend an unscrupulous asshole.

Since that day, about three years ago, the two have avoided each other.

Henry was mostly busy in Barcelona anyway and, despite the aforementioned dispute, was not angry with Jean.

He knew that Jean would get in touch with him again at some point. And he was right.

It was just noon when Mercedes and Juan Falgas pulled up in front of the hospital building. Head nurse Rita was already waiting for them and quickly led them to Dr. Kremer's office.

"Hola Señora y Señor Falgas. I am delighted to welcome you both here. How can I help you?" Eugenio Kremer was buttering them up, and he was doing it well. He was especially taken with the beautiful Mercedes, whom he had only spoken to on the phone before. This earned him a few strange looks from Rita.

Juan ignored Eugenio's embarrassing courtship behavior, and when Mercedes mentioned that she would like to look around the hospital, he was somehow relieved.

Even head nurse Rita managed a smile and assured her how much she would enjoy showing Señora Falgas around.

When the two women had left, Juan took a quick sip of his coffee and then turned to the doctor without further ado.

"Doctor, what have you been up to since our last phone call?"

Eugenio Kremer began to grin and reached under his desk to retrieve a package.

"That's the €250,000 I mentioned. My people have been busy," he said proudly. But when Falgas reached for the package, he pulled it back.

"Not so fast. First tell me what you think of my proposal, señor!"

"What's with the shell game, Doctor? We agreed that the Colombian thing was getting too dangerous! You released all those people, didn't you?"

"After all, you promised me that the poor bastards would be shipped back to fucking Colombia."

Eugenio Kremer was still grinning.

"No, I'm afraid I have to disappoint you, jefe. I really didn't see the point in that, and besides, I even increased our quota, hahaha!"

"You did what?" Juan Falgas was about to explode.

"You understood me perfectly, Señor Falgas," said the doctor defiantly.

"After all, business is fantastic right now. I see absolutely no reason to change anything else. I'll continue as before, even if you suddenly decide to become a humanitarian!

Besides, I called you here for a completely different matter. In principle, that's what this is all about!"

"What kind of garbage are you talking about, Eugenio?" Juan Falgas was about to jump over the desk.

"It's not garbage, damn it! It's just that from your side, this shit could blow up in our faces. Your wife is a damn security risk for us, and you know it!"

"What are you trying to tell me, man? Are you telling me to kill my wife?"

Juan Falgas thought Eugenio's statement was a bad joke and noticed that his pulse was beginning to race.

"Exactly, jefe. That's exactly what you're going to do today if you've got any balls, understand ... hahaha." Eugenio's laughter suddenly took on a diabolical tone.

Of course, Juan had thought about it, but actually doing it was another matter.

Besides, there was one small detail. Just milliseconds before he lunged across the desk and grabbed his employee by the throat, he remembered.

Sure, sometimes he could kill his Mercedes, but no matter what she did to him, he still loved her with all his heart.

"Damn pig, you nasty ..." Suddenly, the office door opened and Mercedes and Nurse Rita stood in the room, looking terrified.

When Juan let go of the doctor's throat and heard his wife screaming, still furious, he suddenly saw stars.

Everything around him turned pitch black.

"Thank God you're here." Eugenio put the gold-plated Buddha back on the table.

"Dear Señora, your husband has gone mad. He wanted to kill you here in Vidasacra. That was his plan! When I said something and tried to change his mind, he attacked me too."

After Eugenio Kremer had fed his boss one lie after another, two nurses came in and wheeled the unconscious man out of the office.

When Mercedes saw her husband in this pitiful state, she suddenly felt free and finally ready to face the rest of her life alone.

"Now, please take a seat. Would you like a cognac to help you recover from the shock, Señora?" When Mercedes smiled and nodded, the doctor's face lit up again. However, he occasionally grimaced in pain, especially while massaging his somewhat maltreated neck.

Juan Falgas regained consciousness to find himself handcuffed and shackled to a kind of bare platform.

The room was dark, and it took him quite a while to collect his thoughts.

Suddenly, Juan realized he wasn't alone in the room. A woman was crying softly. For a moment, he thought it was his wife Mercedes.

Had that damned doctor Kremer simply locked them both in this dungeon? But Falgas quickly realized that it wasn't his wife.

"Who are you?" Juan's voice gave him a headache.

It took a few seconds, then someone replied quietly.

"My name is Elena, and who are you?"

"Juan ... Juan Falgas."

The woman, who was lying about six feet away from him, laughed painfully.

"Juan Falgas, the big construction contractor and financier of this hellhole! Hahaha. You messed with your best employee, huh? And the best part is, we're both in the same shit here, and they're going to kill us, señor!"

After Elena and Juan had introduced themselves in this predicament, the contractor suddenly had an idea, despite his immense headache.

As the five men set off for the Pyrenees, a million and one thoughts raced through Jean's mind. Shortly before leaving Empuriabrava, however, many things had fallen into place.

Henry was looking at various maps on his smartphone and had also found an old map in the door pocket.

"This Vidasacra is near the place where we went hunting together, isn't it?"

"Damn, yes... of course! Then I have an idea, Henry."

Henry looked a little confused, and the other three men suddenly fell silent.

Just a few minutes after Jean had informed his companions, Henry was on the phone again.

"Damn, Jean. We're so lucky! Let's go hunting, hahahahaha... the local hunting club is on a bus tour with heavy drinking for almost a week. That means we can take our hunting gear with us and won't stand out up there."

"Estupendo amigo! But now comes the best part, Hombre!" Jean grinned from ear to ear.

"The hunting lodge where we stayed back then is only about two miles away from the Pedro Leon Hospital!"

"Fuck, you can't get much luckier than that!"

The men laughed.

CHAPTER 12: *on the hunt*

During the drive to the Pyrenees, Henry fiddled with the car radio. He couldn't find a station that suited his taste in music. Jean found this extremely annoying. But then he found a small MP3 stick, which he inserted into the appropriate slot on the car radio. Suddenly, AC/DC's "Thunderstruck" blared out and the men sang along. "Na Na Na Na Na Na Na Na Na ... Thunder ... Na Na Na Na Na Na

Na Na Na ... Thunder ...

It was a good song to get pumped up to. Henry and Jean used to listen to hard rock and heavy metal before every mission.

Some of their comrades took stimulants before going into battle. But Henry and Jean always had a tune in their head. They preferred to get pumped up before a fight with music by Judas Priest, Accept, Iron Maiden, or AC/DC.

A few hours later, Louis, Luca, Pascal, Henry, and Jean reached the hunting lodge in the forest. Henry almost wrecked their vehicle on the way there.

The motorhome skidded on the muddy dirt road. It just managed to slide between two massive pine trees. After the men got out, little Louis dropped to his knees and spread his arms. The others just stared at him in disbelief.

"What's the matter, guys? Enjoy the forest air! So healthy, so pure and clear!" He didn't get any further, because Henry kicked him so hard that his face kissed the forest floor. While everyone laughed and Louis saw only Henry's white teeth as he fumed, Jean Sarre lit a cigarette and took a deep, satisfying drag.

"Well, well, Señor Louis ... Healthy, pure air! Mierda ... Hombre, we're not here on vacation, we have work to do, understand?"

"Si Señor, lo siento! I'm sorry!"

"Come on, Louis, don't shit your overalls!" Everyone laughed, except for the small, stocky man who was still lying on the ground.

"As long as you don't screw everything up with your jokes..."

Now Louis had to laugh too, whereupon Henry reached out his hand to help him up.

Meanwhile, Elena was fiddling with Juan Falgas' pants in the pitch-dark room. "Damn it, stop twitching, man!"
Juan tried to wriggle free, giggling, but the restraints prevented him.
"Hahahaaahiii ... you got it, you must feel it, Señora?"
Elena patted his buttocks as best she could.
"Further forward, the hard part, Señora!" Falgas giggled again.
"Damn it, you're tickling me, hihihi!"
Elena soon lost patience. But now she felt something hard and hoped fervently that it was what she was looking for.

The old hunting lodge was incredibly spacious. Henry and Jean still remembered it vaguely from when the hunting party had stopped there. What an amazing coincidence that the local hunters were out on the prowl in Paris.
Jean decided that there was no time to lose, so he consulted with Henry and Pascal.
"Listen," he said quietly, while Louis and Luca were still arguing loudly about where to sleep.
"Henry, please do me a favor and keep an eye on our two Spanish friends! Pascal and I want to get as close to the hospital as possible to check out the situation. Judging by the map, or rather Pascal's story, we should only have to go through the forest to the river to finally reach the back of the building!" Pascal Cortez nodded.

"Exactly, Jean, if we can get there, that's the only way we'll get to the hospital unmolested. Let's get on with it. The big problem is still the guards. As soon as we go in, we're sure to have visitors."

Luca had meanwhile ended his argument with Louis and interrupted Pascal grumpily.

"If one of us goes, we all go!"

But when Jean promised the landlord that Pascal and he couldn't do anything without his help anyway and that it was only a matter of a situation assessment, the giant quickly calmed down again.

Thank God, almost all the uncertainties had now been cleared up. Finally, Pascal and Jean could set off in their hunting gear.

The hospital was located west of the hunting lodge. The two men first had to pass through a forest of beech and Pyrenean pine trees.

Suddenly, there was a loud crack in the undergrowth. Both Pascal and Jean stopped in their tracks.

"Damn, what was that? Why didn't we bring any weapons? Mierda, damn it! There are definitely wolves here, and I don't even have a knife!" Pascal was really freaking out; his voice was shaking a little. Jean Sarre had to suppress a laugh.

"Stay cool, big shot! I haven't seen any wolves or bears here, but there are plenty of wild boars!"

As if to prove his point, Jean knelt down to take a closer look.

"Look here! See that trail? Those footprints are from a large wild boar, look!"

Pascal looked at the tracks and wasn't really reassured.

"That must be a real monster, judging by the size of its shoes," he remarked dryly. "Do these creatures attack people? If so, then cheers!"

Jean tried to calm Pascal, who was still swallowing hard. He explained that wild boars were extremely shy and that incidents involving humans were rare. Only someone who got between a wild boar mother, known as a sow, and her piglets would be in real trouble. That had to suffice as reassurance, because they still had a bit of a way to go.

What he didn't tell his companion was that he now had a strange feeling in the pit of his stomach. The enormous size and depth of the tracks indicated a very large boar. It must have weighed well over 150 kilograms (330 lbs), maybe even more.

No, he had seen huge black boars before. Besides, he could read tracks and trails, but he had never come across such large and deep prints. The pig must have been abnormally large.

After leaving the dark coniferous forest behind them, they reached a small rocky outcrop.

The men had already heard the roar of the river below for some time.

The noise was so loud that Pascal had to shout to his companion.

"Look, the completely wrecked ambulance, over there!

They've already pulled it out of the river. It's still standing over there, right behind the hospital, in the large parking lot."

Sarre opened his backpack and took out a telescope, which he unfolded. Pascal watched him with interest.

"High tech, huh?"

Jean didn't respond and looked through the telescope intently.

The flowing river was the first obstacle, but thankfully it wasn't that wide everywhere. A little further upstream, it would be possible to cross, where it meandered towards the hospital.

Then came the next obstacle: the parking lot.

Open terrain and hardly any camouflage to get behind the hospital unnoticed.

The third, but certainly not the last, obstacle would be the back doors themselves. They were definitely made of steel and burglar-proof. What's more, there were cameras installed above the two back doors.

"Great, we'll have to shoot them," Jean remarked, looking in Pascal's direction, who was covering his ears.

"What?" The loud thunder and roar of the river drowned out every word.

After Jean had seen enough for the moment, he folded up his spective and took a few photos with his digital camera.

Pascal said something again. In response, Jean pointed toward the forest. The two of them left the rock.

Two hundred meters further on, the men were able to talk to each other again.

"Damn, that was loud, hombre," Pascal complained.

"You can't have everything, amigo! Besides, you've already made acquaintance with the river. Come on, let's keep going in this direction! I want to see the other side of the hospital. Maybe it's easier from there? At least, I hope so."

So they walked a little further through the forest when Pascal suddenly grabbed his sleeve and whispered.

"Look, down there in the hollow. Those wild animals are wallowing in the mud. Are those the ones? You know, the ones with the tracks?"

Jean shook his head. The herd of wild boars, consisting of twenty animals at the front, had not yet noticed the men.

"No, señor. First of all, that was a trail, not a track. I'll explain the difference another time. And secondly, the ones down there are much too small for footprints like that!"

"Too small, you want to kid me, you smartass? Too small? I know big Rottweilers that are smaller than some of those pigs down there!"

Now the herd, or rather the lead sow, had caught wind of the two men and disappeared loudly, snorting in the undergrowth.

"Come on, you coward, we have to keep going, damn it!" Jean grinned broadly. Once Pascal had regained his composure, they were able to continue.

The men trudged toward the noise again, and this time they had better luck.

When Jean had a clear view, he saw what he had hoped to see.

Down below, he could see one side of the building and the gatehouse, and there was also a small bridge leading over the river.

"Estupendo!" Jean rejoiced. 'That's exactly how it has to be. From here, we can see everything, cross the river unharmed, and sneak past the building on the side!"

"And we can count the guards," Pascal remarked, not quite as euphoric.

"Brilliant, mate! At least you're thinking!"

Pascal Cortez smiled, revealing his rotten teeth.

Finally, some recognition. Even from their leader.

That went down like a treat.

Jean took a few photos, then turned back to Pascal, who was still grinning.

"We've seen enough for now. Let's go back to the cabin! I can think about it there, and I'm thirsty now. Plus, my nicotine addiction is kicking in!"

"You can have one of mine," said Cortez, but Jean declined, pointing out to his companion that smoking in the forest could end badly.

So Pascal obediently put his cigarettes back in his pocket and followed Sarre, but not without first shaking his head demonstratively and groaning loudly.

The return trip to the forest hut was quicker than the way there.

Cortez would certainly not have found his way out of the fairy-tale forest on his own. He would probably have gotten so lost that he would have ended up starving to death.

He trotted admiringly behind Jean like a young puppy. Jean Sarre, on the other hand, only glanced occasionally at a small compass. The former legionnaire moved quite elegantly even on the rocky and partly muddy ground. Well, if you ignored his small belly and his shortness of breath caused by nicotine consumption.

These were some of the advantages of his former military service and his missions.

Well, every cloud has a silver lining. At least that was usually the case.

Shortly before arriving at their forest hut, the men encountered wild animals again.

This time, they startled two deer, which ran away barking loudly.

"I didn't know pigs could trumpet like elephants and deer could bark. They sound almost like dogs!"

"Yes, my friend, there's a lot you don't know. When we get through all this shit and survive..."

"Exactly, Jean, when we get the money from that sadistic doctor, the first thing I'm going to do is buy a book and..."

"No, hombre, I'll give you that. I'll buy you a smart book about the fauna and flora of the forest, cabrón!"

Both had to laugh, but their good mood didn't last long. Pascal's face suddenly darkened.

"No, fuck the money. Damn it, that's not what this is about! I want that doctor. I want to execute the dirty pig who killed my brother. I'm doing this for Fernando. But a simple bullet in the head is far too good for that asshole. He should suffer for a long time. I want to see that pig suffer. Please promise me you'll help me, Jean! Please, promise me!" Pascal had tears in his eyes.

"Agreed, amigo! But now let's go back," replied Jean, patting his companion on the shoulder in a friendly manner.

Less than five minutes later, the hunting lodge was finally in sight again and Pascal's pulse had stabilized.

Outside the lodge, three men were sitting around a small table playing cards.

"You're cheating us, you damn ... Ni ... black devil, aren't you?" Henry grinned from ear to ear, and with all the money he had won at poker the last few times, he didn't even hear Lucas' racist insults.

"Aaah, here come our lost brothers," Louis remarked briefly as he sorted his cards.

"That's enough, I'm outta here, hombres." Luca stood up and walked over to Jean and Pascal.

Luca eyed Jean for a moment, then couldn't hold back his question any longer. "Hey Jean, how did you end up in the Foreign Legion? What's your story, cabrón?"

Jean flinched briefly, but after his former legionnaire comrade Henry nodded encouragingly, he told those present his adventurous story.

CHAPTER 13: *Sins of the past*

Jean Sarre, who had a completely different name back then, had fallen in love with a girl named Yvonne. He was young and even toyed with the idea of building a future with his girlfriend.
The two were in the early days of their relationship, but Yvonne, who was usually always cheerful, had another side to her.
As soon as things got physical, the blonde woman, who was just under 5 feet tall, freaked out terribly. She became downright hysterical and rejected Jean not only verbally. Jean was quite confused by this, but decided to just give her time to take this step. But every time the two wanted to sleep together, the most beautiful thing in the world ended in disaster. On the fifth or sixth attempt, the situation escalated completely.
Once again, they had kissed tenderly and ended up in Yvonne's bed. But when Jean wanted to penetrate his girlfriend, Yvonne mutated from Dr. Jekyll to Mr. Hyde. In no time at all, she developed a multiple personality. She bit, kicked, and beat him.
He took a beating and tried to hold his girlfriend by her arms and wrists, but Yvonne was so out of control that she bit his right breast until it bled while ramming her knee into his genitals.

Moaning in pain, Jean rolled out of bed. On the cold linoleum floor, he tried to make sense of what had just happened, cursing under his breath. Yvonne was convulsing. A few minutes later, the young woman began to cry uncontrollably.

When both had calmed down somewhat, Yvonne explained to her boyfriend the reason for her trauma.

Until recently, her stepfather had sexually abused her several times a week, but her mother turned a blind eye and a deaf ear. She simply didn't believe her daughter because it couldn't be true!

Jean listened to Yvonne. He let her talk without interrupting her. His own injuries and his swollen testicles were not the focus now. The more and the longer Yvonne talked, the angrier he became. After this tell-all, Jean no longer felt his own pain. But somewhere inside him, there was a burning, searing pain. It was pure hatred for this man that hurt him inside.

After the conversation, the two cuddled lovingly, holding each other tight as if they were drowning.

Yvonne was completely distraught and begged him not to do anything. But he couldn't, or rather, wouldn't give her that promise.

Secretly, Jean had long since decided to confront this bastard. He didn't give much thought to the consequences of this inevitable confrontation. He was simply too angry.

Even if Yvonne's stepfather was such an "important man" in this stuffy little town, he couldn't get away with something like this. But why wouldn't her mother believe her? It made no sense to Jean. Just because otherwise her whole "perfect world" would have collapsed.

When he got home, there was no one Jean could talk to about it. His parents weren't there, but even if they had been, what would they have advised him to do? Probably that it wasn't his business and that only Yvonne could report her stepfather. That he should just stay out of it. That's most likely what they would have told him.

But for the young, impulsive man, that was not an option.

Franz Xaver Schanzelsberger was a large, powerful man who was reasonably well-liked. However, he couldn't care less about the concerns and wishes of those around him.

The mayor and local politician was a master of hypocrisy and manipulation.

This made Schanzelsberger very popular with his voters, even though he often humiliated his subordinates and his family.

Franz was a very extroverted but also socially incompatible individual. He took even the slightest criticism of himself as a deep insult. He usually reacted to this with a fit of rage.

There was no question that Franz Xaver Schanzelsberger was a pathological narcissist.

Every Wednesday evening, Franz could be found in the village pub. Sometimes he went there to play cards, but most of the time he could be found in the bowling alley in the basement.

This was also the case on this particular Wednesday, when both his life and the life of young Jean Sarre were about to change dramatically.

Franz was having a bad night. On top of that, he was annoyed by the provocative comments of his bowling buddies. After all, he was the president of the local bowling club, "Gut Holz." But when he threw his second "lame duck" of the night, he was close to throwing the ball into the gutter and heading straight home.

Normally, he was more of a "nine-pin" bowler, but today nothing was going right for him.

Franz had to put up with another stupid remark from his fellow ninepin bowlers. He downed his bottle of beer and left immediately without saying goodbye.

Outside, in the more or less poorly lit parking lot, stood his Mercedes G-Class. He reached into his pocket, pulled out his car keys, and was about to press the button to unlock the doors when someone grabbed him by the shoulder.

Franz dropped the car keys in shock.

"Hey, damn it! What the hell, asshole?"

In the semi-darkness, he could make out a young man.

"Who are you and what do you want, kid?"

"Schanzelsberger, what kind of nasty asshole are you?" Jean hissed at the man, full of rage.

"You're getting your perverted hands on your stepdaughter, you sick pig!"

Franz was visibly shocked by these true words. He had threatened to kill Yvonne if she ever revealed their secret.

In his eyes, Yvonne was somehow to blame for the whole thing. Why did she always have to run around his apartment dressed so skimpily? Besides, everyone else was to blame, except him. After all, he was the undisputed boss of this cursed village.

"Shut up and piss off, you stupid fucking brat! Don't talk shit!"

"How dare you accuse me of such a thing?"

"You little coward, who do you think you are?"

Jean remained silent.

"Your time is up!"

"Get out of here, you little wanker!"

Jean didn't move an inch.

"You'll pay for this! Your position and honor will be gone. Once your people find out what a sick pedophile you are, they'll chase you out of your own village! Want to bet?"

Franz was shaking all over. He felt nothing but uncontrollable rage toward the boy in front of him. Twenty-year-old Jean was still standing only about two meters away from him. He made no move to leave.

Then suddenly Franz saw red and lunged at the lad.

He grabbed Jean by the throat with both hands to strangle him. But Jean kicked him in the groin, freed himself from his grip, and then kicked him in the kneecap.

Franz groaned and yelped, but he remained in attack mode and tried to grab his adversary.

He lunged forward, slipped, and stumbled to the ground.

He fell so badly that he hit his head on a curb. Skull fracture! His eyes glazed over and blood ran into the gutter.

Seconds later, the man was dead. Franz Xaver Schanzelsberger had lost his life in the parking lot of his favorite bar.

Jean stood there frozen. He didn't move again until someone screamed hysterically at him.

"You murderer! I saw it with my own eyes. You killed him. You're going to jail for this!"

Jean heard the words, but they sounded as if they were coming through a wall of cotton wool.

Completely paralyzed, he gave in to a reflex that was only too human: the urge to flee.

He ran to his tornado-red Golf Diesel and sped away. He had to get away quickly, far away, because there was one thing he didn't want: to go to prison. At some point that night, he made up his mind. He parked his old car several hundred meters away from his parents' house so he could sneak back there like a thief in the night.

His parents were currently on a cruise, so they couldn't be reached. They would probably have advised him to turn himself in anyway. After all, they believed in justice, although their naivety had caused a few family disputes in the past.

Jean was neither an optimist nor a pessimist. When he saw two police cars turning into his street, he knew, as a realist, that they were looking for him. He would not be able to pack his bags or leave a farewell letter.

The risk of being arrested was immense.

Spending years in prison for manslaughter was really not an option for him. It was an accident, but who would believe him? The events of that damn night were about to destroy his whole life.

When he was back on the road, despite his tear-stained eyes, he had a clear goal. Knowing that he wouldn't be able to contact his family and friends for the foreseeable future, perhaps even for years, he drove through a city that was foreign to him at dawn.

After leaving a small roundabout, he parked his car on Rue d'Ostende. Completely exhausted and mentally torn, he stood in front of the recruitment office of the Foreign Legion in Strasbourg.

After this story, there was silence at first. The four men had listened attentively, and then Luca broke the silence.

"Jean, amigo, I probably would have done the same thing. I respect your honesty. Do you know how your family and Yvonne are doing today?"

"Yvonne took her own life a month later. My parents died in an accident two months after that. Is there anything else you want to know, Luca?"

Luca shook his head, his face reddening. He realized he had asked one question too many. Meanwhile, Henry took five cans of San Miguel out of the cooler and handed them around.

Jean wasted no time and showed the photos he had taken on a small laptop.

The five men then discussed the matter loudly.

"Mierda. Damn it ... Hey guys, let Jean finish first!"

Henry tried to at least steer the chaos in an orderly direction.

After some discussion, the men finally agreed that Jean would be in charge of this mission. Finally, Henry praised his former comrade-in-arms in the highest terms.

Even the eccentric Luca couldn't argue with that.

"So who's going to take out the guards?"

"No one," Jean replied.

"I still have to think about that, Luca.

I want as few people as possible to be killed during the operation.

But I think I already have a solution."

Now it was Jean's turn to play poker.

Because, overall, he didn't have a precise plan yet. But he would never admit that.

Besides, he was thinking about the beautiful Elena, who had betrayed him so badly. Maybe he would see her again soon, and then that Mercedes Falgas ... What was she doing right now?

Señora Falgas was still a little unsettled. Perhaps it had something to do with the way Doctor Kremer was staring at her with his little eyes.

Somehow, the whole situation reminded her of a movie. That animated film she had recently seen on a streaming platform.

She thought about it for a few seconds, but then the title suddenly came to her. "The Jungle Book." Specifically, the scene where the snake Ka tried to hypnotize the little human child Mowgli and succeeded.

Yes, with the difference that these Disney films always had a happy ending.

Mercedes Falgas had to stand her ground. She couldn't show any fear in front of this unpleasant slaughterer. No, quite the opposite! She had to act confident and demonstrate to this lunatic that she was in control.

"So, Doctor, what have you done since our last phone call?" Finally, she had broken the uncomfortable silence in the stuffy office.

The doctor snorted softly, rubbing his almost non-existent neck for the umpteenth time.

"Well, señora. We have everything under control here. You don't need to worry about a thing. Besides... I have something else for you!"

Eugenio Kremer reached under his desk to slide the package across it again.

"There's two hundred and fifty thousand in there!"

Mercedes cleared her throat.

"And soon you'll get just as much again, maybe even more; well, is that something, Señora? After all, I hear that the construction business isn't exactly booming at the moment! It's no secret that the construction industry has been in crisis for a long time. After all, you want to maintain your standard of living, don't you?"

He had done it.

Mercedes Falgas drank the cognac in one gulp. Then she placed the glass on the hardwood table in front of her and reached for the package without shame.

"Estupendo, Señora Falgas! Then I guess we're business partners now, hahaha..."

Mercedes was still paralyzed. At last she was no longer under the thumb of her violent husband.

Now she was free! After all those sad years, she could finally live her own life. But at what price?

What would happen to Juan? Would they kill him? What should she tell the police? An accident... a heart attack? She tried to push the thought out of her mind, but with little success.

"Listen, Doctor Kremer! You warned me about my husband back then. In return, I told you about that snoop and his CD. You also promised me you would treat those Colombians humanely. I hope you keep your promise!"

The doctor poured his new business partner another cognac and cleared his throat quietly.

"But of course, Señora. Don't forget about that journalist Brieaux. We both nurtured that snake!" The doctor winked cheekily and continued talking. "I keep my promises and, as I said, all you have to do is keep up appearances. That's all. From now on, I'll do business exclusively with you. As for your husband, we'll find a solution! A humane one, of course!"

Doctor Eugenio Kremer tried to smile particularly nicely, but Mercedes saw only a diabolical grimace.

Then the phone rang, and before the Doc picked up the receiver, he put his hand on Mercedes' shoulder. "Everything will be fine, Señora. Trust me! After this call, we'll have one less problem!"

Jean and his companions had decided to check out the front of the hospital.

Pascal and Jean had to stay in the background. After all, there was a risk that the two of them would be recognized.

So Louis, Luca, and Henry sat in the driver's cab, while Jean and Pascal made themselves comfortable in the back of the motorhome. They tried desperately to see outside through the curtains.

"Hey Henry, are we in Vidasacra yet?"

"No, amigo, but wait... I can see it... There's the town sign!"

Now they were driving past a cemetery. A short time later, they approached a large, green-painted building.

"This must be it, right?"

"Si!" Pascal remarked, "The Devil's Hospital!"

"Pull over to the right, Henry," said Jean.

"Remember, we're tourists. We mustn't attract the attention of the guards, men!"

Henry wanted to park the motorhome on the right-hand side of the road, but a man wearing a yellow helmet and a high-vis vest began waving frantically.

Henry rolled down the window as the construction worker ran toward the motorhome, waving his arms.

"You can't stay there, señores!"

"You can't park here, señor! We're working on the road and need to park the construction trailer there!"

Henry nodded politely and started the car again. But the construction worker, now waving back cheerfully, simply stood in front of the car.

"Listen, brother! There's a small parking lot up ahead, above the cemetery. You can stay there overnight if you want."

"Thanks, brother," Henry replied to the man.

"Road construction is a tough job, isn't it? How long have you been working here?"

The black man grinned broadly, pleased that there were still people who appreciated his sweaty profession.

"Well, you're right! We've already torn up the road up at the hospital because we have to lay new water pipes. But it's almost quitting time!

Today, we're just going to park the construction trailer in front of the hospital and continue the day after tomorrow. Then we have to work fast because the entire hospital has no water while we're working. But tomorrow the construction crew has the day off! We've earned it!"

"Estupendo, amigo, well then, we wish you a nice day off and keep up the good work, adios!"

"Adiós," replied the man with a laugh as Henry turned the car around.

After parking the motorhome in the small cemetery parking lot, the five men were able to stretch their legs.

"Seven!" Jean looked at the display of his digital camera.

"What... seven?" asked Luca, looking a little irritated.

"There are seven guards in the photo I just took. Damn, maybe there are even more?"

Jean scratched his head, making Luca laugh. "Well, what's our great military strategist planning to do about that?"

Lucas's provocative grin and his taunting remarks were getting on Jean's nerves. But instead of responding, he turned away and walked a few meters to think.

CHAPTER 14: *Prayer before the attack*

At the cemetery entrance stood an oversized, weathered statue of the Virgin Mary, her arm, stained with bird droppings, pointing toward the hospital. Two old tin cans, one containing candles, the other small change, stood forlornly at her base.

As if drawn by a magnet, Jean moved toward her. At the same time, he began searching his pockets for coins.

Meanwhile, the other men chatted in front of the motorhome, once again making fun of poor Louis and his torn overalls.

Jean threw a coin into the dented tin can and then took a candle from the other one, which he immediately lit and carefully placed at the base of the Madonna statue.

A thousand thoughts raced through his mind once again. If only he had, then they wouldn't have to...!

The narrow, white candle burned, its flame blazing bright egg yolk yellow and straight up.

Why straight up, actually? The flame should at least flicker, because there was a slight breeze blowing!

Jean Sarre knelt before the statue of Mary and suddenly felt exhausted.

Suddenly, he noticed a coin that someone must have placed on the pedestal. It was a silver coin that still glowed strangely in the evening sun.

Then he felt a hand on his left shoulder, heard a familiar voice, and shuddered.

"Well, my son, look at us again!"

Jean wanted to turn around, but he couldn't. Somehow he felt as if he had just turned into a pillar of salt.

He hadn't heard her come. The old woman dressed in raven black suddenly stood in front of the weathered statue of Mary, holding the shiny silver coin in her hand.

"I knew you would show up, Jean. You haven't disappointed me. Now take the silver coin that, thank God, you left behind on the church square in Cadaqués! It will help you now, even though about two thousand years ago, this coin brought anything but luck to a man named Judas and his friends. But in the end, you must give this silver coin to your enemy. Please remember that!"

Jean sighed and began to sweat as the old woman slipped the silver coin into his shirt pocket.

The expert tried to wake up from this trance, but he just couldn't.

"Don't resist, my dear Jean, and pray to Saint Jude Thaddeus before the fight. He will watch over you tonight," said the little grandmother with snow-white hair softly.

"Oh Jean ... after all these many, many years, I'm becoming forgetful and a real grandmother, a real abuela, even though my son never became a father. You still need a silver coin. After all, you're dealing with two real devils!

I will watch over you, but tonight is the night of nights, and you must do it today!"

Granny placed her bony hand on his forehead and slipped another coin into his shirt pocket. Jean then saw a film running in fast motion before his inner eye. When the old woman withdrew her hand, the vision ended.

"Oh, one more thing. You promised your comrade Pascal something. Remember that! But leave it to nature! It will avenge you."

Jean didn't understand and tried to shrug his shoulders, but it didn't work.

The old woman smiled mildly, leaned over the man, and kissed him tenderly on the forehead. Then she was gone again.

Jean awoke from his trance when someone spoke to him and tapped him on the shoulder.

"Hey, don't sleep... wake up, hombre!"

At about the same time, Elena laboriously cut through the ropes that were supposed to restrain Juan Falgas on the cot with a small pocket knife.

Meanwhile, Señora Mercedes Falgas asked to see Eugenio Kremer's notes and was quite astonished.

"Well, there you have it, Señora, your husband doesn't have a clue about making money, does he?"

Mercedes looked up and smiled. Her roe-brown eyes changed color. Slowly, they grew darker and darker, almost black.

"Last week we performed five transplants, and three more are planned for tomorrow alone!"

The doctor held up his "business plan" proudly, looking like a little kid who had just won the raffle.

"We have a money-printing machine here, Señora Falgas!"

"A gold mine, yes, that's even better!"

Kremer became more and more caught up in his own euphoria. He looked like he was on drugs.

"Just look at the revenue, Señora!"

"Look, look!"

"Well," Mercedes Falgas remarked dryly. 'But Doctor, what about the other people who know about this? Have you taken care of Sarre?"

"Claro, Señora! He should be dead by now."

"What do you mean, 'should be'?" Mercedes replied.

"No, Señora, we took care of it and I've been notified. The man is dead!"

"The whole thing wasn't cheap, of course, but Jean Sarre had a regrettable surfing accident off Fuerteventura a few days ago. It's a terrible thing, Señora, but maybe he would have wanted a burial at sea. Although probably not as fish food."

A few hundred meters further on, five men sat in an old construction trailer, knowing that tonight was the night.

"So, hombres! We don't have many options left. But giving

up now and leaving the Colombian people to their terrible fate is not an option," said Jean, and the others nodded in agreement.

Jean explained his plan to the men, and what secretly surprised him was that there was so little opposition.

Only Luca grimaced briefly, but when Henry cleared his throat and nodded in agreement, the fence and pseudogastronome from Figueres held back.

"So Luca and Louis are supposed to get us into this Fort Knox-style hospital," said Henry. 'Do you really think that's a good idea, Jean?' Why did Henry involuntarily think of 'Dumb and Dumber' when he heard that? Louis and Luca now really looked like Spanish road workers. Even Louis' torn overalls now fit the part.

They found some high-visibility vests and hard hats in the construction trailer, and once Pascal, Henry, and Jean were mostly satisfied with the two men's outfits, they gave them their final instructions.

"So, ... after we've cut off the water supply to the hospital, you two take the toolbox and get going. Everything has to be done quickly, so no one gets suspicious.

Tell the guards that you need to inspect the main pipes in the building and that it will be done quickly.

When you're in the basement, just open the rear security door for us. As soon as we're inside, we'll take care of the whole clan and free the prisoners."

"What weapons are we taking, Sarre?" 'None,' Jean replied to the man from Figueres. Luca raised his eyebrows and was about to complain.

"The guards will search you, the risk is too great and that would completely ruin the element of surprise!" Henry and Pascal nodded in agreement.

"As soon as we're inside, you'll get your weapons, and that's final!"

"Can I at least take a knife?" Luca almost begged Jean. "You can take a box cutter. Anything else would be too conspicuous."

After Jean's statement, Luca looked a little calmer.

"Henry and I will shoot out the cameras and the rear lights when you two have been in the building for fifteen minutes. The guards and staff mustn't know what they're up against."

Henry nodded in agreement and looked at Jean for a long time.

He wasn't actually a very religious man, but before a dangerous mission, a prayer couldn't hurt. Since that special operation in Africa, even he prayed from time to time and almost always wore his amulet as a talisman.

"Jean, shall we pray before we leave?"

The expert and former legionnaire agreed and rummaged for a yellowed piece of paper in his wallet. He had written it years ago. Jean remembered the old woman's words and began to read the prayer aloud:

Holy patron saint Judas Thaddeus.

You faithful and glorious apostle and companion of our Lord.

Hear my voice and my intercession.

Protect me from all attacks of the evil enemy. See my suffering and come to my aid, as I implore you.

Saint Judas Thaddeus, have mercy on me.

Save me from my greatest distress, and even if the shadow of death hangs over me, I will fear no evil as long as you are at my side.

Protect me, help me, and save me even from hopeless situations.

Saint Jude Thaddeus, have mercy on me.

Sadness and misfortune have surrounded me.

Even in the most difficult situations, you still bring help.

Saint Jude, hear my voice.

Amen.

"Amen," replied Pascal and Henry, shaking hands.

Luca wouldn't be Luca if he didn't make fun of it.

He whispered something in Louis's ear, and the two of them laughed.

Shortly before sunset, the five men set off. All equipped with walkie-talkies, Louis and Luca, the "road workers," with blue toolboxes, and the remaining three in camouflage hunting gear and heavily armed.

Luca couldn't bear to watch as the small, chubby Louis struggled with the valve. "Leave me alone, you son of a bitch, it's a miracle you're still alive!" With a jerk of the valve, Luca sabotaged the water supply to the "Pedro Leon" clinic.

The three remaining men were just walking through the small pine forest and looking down at the rear parking lot of the clinic.

The building really didn't look like a hospital, but more like a high-security prison.

Dusk was slowly falling, and Jean and his two comrades needed a little more light to get across the small bridge unharmed and, above all, without using flashlights.

"Once we're across the footbridge, we'll sneak past the building and hide behind the boulder next to the big pine tree. From there, we'll have a good shooting position and we'll be at the back door quickly."

Jean looked at his wristwatch.

"We have to hurry. Luca and Louis should be opening the security door in half an hour, and then the fun begins!"

"But leave that fat doctor to me. I want to see him suffer for my brother Fernando."

Jean nodded. The men had to shout to hear each other over the roaring mountain river.

In the meantime, Elena had managed to free herself and Juan Falgas from their bonds, and after they had gotten their bearings in the pitch-black room, Elena tried to pick the locked door with Juan's small pocket knife.

"Can't you do that faster? I thought people in your line of work could do things like that." Jean raged, but Elena ignored him and kept trying.

"Strictly speaking, I didn't need your services at all! I even had to blow up Jean Sarre's car myself. The bomb was supposed to explode when that stupid guy got in. But that weird mutt in the back must have triggered the motion sensor by jumping around."

Elena would have loved to cut him into strips with her small knife for that statement, but she kept trying to pick the door lock. In the dark, the Russian woman wouldn't have known where to stab him anyway.

Meanwhile, Louis and Luca were still standing in front of the hospital and were being checked by three guards. The man with the evil stare and the dangerous-looking moustache was doing his best and was really getting into his inspection work. After head nurse Rita also noticed that no water was coming out of her shower and she appeared, fuming and with shampoo in her hair, the two "road workers" were quickly let through.

"What the hell is going on? Why don't we have any water? Fix it right now and next time let us know before you turn off the water or electricity!"

Nurse Rita yelled at the two men at the top of her lungs, her whole body, including her almost exposed breasts, shaking violently.

At the same time, she held her bathrobe tightly closed so as not to stand completely naked in front of the men.

Louis and Luca tried to look understanding and concerned, but this hysterical woman looked like she was ready to explode. Her shampooed hair was sticking out in all directions. "Like an exploded sofa cushion," thought Louis, biting his tongue hard to keep from laughing out loud.

By now it was almost dark and time was running out. Jean, Henry, and Pascal approached the small bridge, which looked extremely dilapidated and anything but safe.

The roaring river below was enough to strike fear into anyone's heart, but Pascal impatiently pushed past Henry and Jean.

"Be careful!" Jean shouted after him, but it was too late. Pascal slipped on the wet, moss-covered beams, lost his grip, and fell.

The only thing Jean and Henry heard from Pascal was a cry of 'Mierda!' Then the Catalan was swept away by the current.

Jean and Henry ran to the embankment and tried to spot Pascal, but he was probably already hundreds of meters away, and the rugged rocks that would have made canoeing impossible on this section of the river would surely break every bone in his body.

"Damn it!" Henry shouted, 'such a clumsy fuck… May he rest in peace,' and crossed himself. Jean had regained his composure and muttered something. "The first time, he was able to cheat fate, but now the river had finally claimed him."

Jean crossed the bridge very carefully, step by step.

When Henry crossed, he almost slipped, but Jean grabbed him by the arm and pulled him out of danger.

This reminded Jean of a situation that had occurred twenty years earlier in a small African village. Since that day, Henry and he had been connected by a supernatural force.

CHAPTER 15: *Africa — the amulet*

The sun was burning like fire at midday. Auguste, Henry, and Jean had been tasked with coordinating with the village police to ensure that the impending rebel attack could be successfully thwarted.

After the three men got out of their SUV, they walked down a dusty road. Well, "road" was probably the wrong word for this collection of potholes.

Suddenly, Jean was hit on the leg by a pebble thrown at them by a small boy. The ten-year-old urchin threw a second pebble in Henry's direction. Then the child turned to an old man dressed in black who called him over.

Auguste, Henry, and Jean watched as the old man scolded the boy and were about to walk on.

Then the little boy shouted something at the men and turned back to the old man.

Now something happened that none of the three foreign legionnaires could have anticipated.

The little boy suddenly had an AK-47 in his hands and tried to aim it at the three men. He waved the weapon like a flag, and the old man literally encouraged the boy to finally shoot.

Auguste immediately drew his pistol from its leather holster and aimed at the child. But before he could pull the trigger,

Henry knocked him down with the butt of his rifle. At the same moment, several shots rang out from the Kalashnikov, but they all hit a house opposite.

Jean took his service weapon and fired. However, he didn't shoot the little boy, but the old man, who was still trying to talk the child down with great emphasis.

The bullet didn't miss its target and hit the old man in the neck.

A fountain of blood spurted high into the air and splattered the dusty street.

The old man didn't even reach for his throat to stop the blood; he just laughed and bared his teeth like a rabid dog.

The little boy saw all the blood, dropped the Kalashnikov in shock, and ran away.

His dirty clothes, mostly blue and white linen rags, were now dotted with red and looked as if they were meant to look that way. As he ran, the rags flapped like flags in the wind.

"Blue, white, and red, the French tricolor," Jean mused for a moment. Something that could easily have passed for a French flag was running away.

Jean and Henry looked at the old man, who was staggering into a doorway. Just before he disappeared, he laughed maliciously once more and made a vulgar gesture toward the legionnaires.

Auguste was completely unaware of what had happened.

He was still lying unconscious in the dust, and Henry felt almost sorry for his ruthless companion.

"Where did all the blood go?" Jean looked questioningly at Henry. Henry just shrugged his shoulders in disbelief. It almost looked as if the dusty African ground had completely absorbed the old man's blood. Not a single drop was to be seen.

Henry wanted to follow the old man, but his comrade held him back by the shoulder.

"Leave the old man alone, my friend! Either you'll find him in some corner or you won't find him anywhere!"

The black man crossed himself.

"That was the devil!" Henry replied.

"Believe me, Jean, we just saw Satan himself!"

"But we won, my friend! The two of us drove him away, Henry!" A slight smile appeared on Sarre's lips.

Suddenly, a figure in a long white caftan appeared behind them.

The elderly woman floated toward Henry and Jean, completely ignoring Auguste lying on the ground.

"Is that an angel?" Henry whispered softly, staring at the woman with wide eyes.

The white cloth of the long caftan fluttered in the wind as the woman stretched out her right hand and held out a silver medallion to Jean.

Jean nodded gratefully to the woman and took it.

Henry also received a medallion from the angelic apparition. He thanked her by kneeling before her and crossing himself again.

Without a word and almost unreal, the white cloths and the person inside disappeared as suddenly as she had come.

"What was that all about?" Jean was the first to find his voice again.

Henry read the inscription on the medallion. "Sanctus Judas Thaddäus."

"Saint Jude, the patron saint of the hopelessly desperate!"

Jean stared at his medallion for a long time. He had received the same one and felt as if he had just awakened from a nightmare.

"We need a patron saint like that, Henry! We need protection like that!"

Now Auguste moved again, looked up, and glared at Jean.

"What the hell happened? Something hit me on the head. Damn it, where's that brat? Did you at least shoot him?"

Auguste tried to get back on his feet, but no one helped him up.

Both Jean and Henry turned away from Auguste in disgust.

Now, in the present, Auguste himself was no longer fit for fish food, but Henry and Jean stood side by side once again, hoping that they would both survive the coming battle.

"Careful, watch out, man," the grim-looking security guard shouted at Louis. But Louis had already stumbled and fallen hard onto the concrete floor of the hospital basement. He just had time to throw the toolbox a few feet away so he wouldn't get hurt by it.

"Tonto ... idiot!" The flying metal box almost hit Luca on the leg.

"How can you be so clumsy?" Luca remarked. Louis picked himself up and looked down at the floor in embarrassment.

"Lo siento, I'm sorry, but why are there so many cables lying around here?" he replied quietly.

The security guard scratched his head briefly and tried hard to look even more unpleasant.

"Just watch where you're stepping, and stay away from the door over there. We had to change something. There are high-voltage cables there. Just do your job, and do it quickly!"

Luca was just thinking about the best angle to stab the security guard in the neck with his carpet knife when the man simply turned away. He then left, saying, "I have to do my rounds now. Let me know when you're done!"

A minute later, Luca and Louis were alone in the small corridor in front of the steel door. Luca tried to use his radio, which of course didn't work.

"Damn it, why would you put an emergency exit under power?"

There had to be at least a lever or a switch somewhere to de-energize the steel door.

"Find the power switch, Louis, and don't look at me like you're stupid. The other three are probably waiting impatiently for us to let them in!"

Louis looked around and actually found a rotary switch, somewhat hidden on the other side of the hallway. However, he wanted to be sure. So he followed the high-voltage cables to the steel door.

"Louis! Now move your ass over there! Turn off the power so I can open this damn door."

Luca was once again seething with rage. Everything had to be done quickly, and Louis couldn't walk and chew gum at the same time, so slowly and carefully did the little, fat man now stroll toward the switch.

At the end of the corridor, a few meters before the emergency exit, there was another narrow door. As Luca passed it, he heard a slight scratching sound behind it.

"Probably mice or rats," he thought, when suddenly the door flew open and hit him hard in the back.

CHAPTER 16: *The chaos begins*

Luca was literally catapulted. With his eyes wide open, he spun around once and saw in a millisecond that Louis was still at least two to three meters away from the power switch. Then it was all over for Luca. He didn't even have time to swear like a trooper one last time. The door had literally grabbed his back and, after the initial contact, wouldn't let go. Luca sizzled like a sausage in the microwave. Smoke came out of every orifice; even his eyeballs seemed to be boiling.

A frantic-looking Juan Falgas stumbled through the open door. When he saw Luca roasting at the emergency exit, he ran up the hallway and past Louis.

In doing so, he accidentally knocked over a guy who was in shock. Not necessarily because he wanted to, but because his eyes had to get used to the light again. After all, he had been locked in a pitch-dark room for a long time.

Louis scrambled to his feet and finally flipped the high-voltage switch. The small red light on the emergency exit stopped flashing.

Unfortunately, that didn't help the dead Luca. Somehow his body now looked like a burst sausage. Smoke and the smell of grilled meat slowly spread through the hallway.

"Smoke on the water," Louis thought for a moment. As a small cloud of smoke rose from the puddle under Lucas' body. After all, that song had been Lucas' favorite.

"How bizarre!" It was as if he had subconsciously known that he would have to die like this someday.

How many times had Louis Sanchez had to listen to that damn song in Luca's bar? Sometimes Louis had the impression that it was the only song in the beat-up jukebox.

Suddenly, the walkie-talkie crackled and the small, stocky Spaniard could hear Jean's voice. "Luca ... Louis ... what are you doing in there, why isn't the emergency exit open yet? We were just about to smash the rear lights, but there was a flash of light and now they're out anyway. Open the damn door!"

Louis pressed the send button on the walkie-talkie. "Luca is dead, the thing was electrified! That fucking doctor had the emergency exit wired for high voltage. Come quickly, I'll open the door for you!"

Louis couldn't think straight anymore. Someone grabbed him from behind and tried to crush his larynx. In a panic, he lashed out, and suddenly the grip on his throat loosened.

The huge guard behind him doubled over in pain. It was only by chance that Louis had hit his groin.

"Louis Sanchez, martial arts expert!" thought the little rascal from Figueres. Now was his moment to triumph and use his infamous karate chop.

The huge security guard with the pockmarked face and black, drooping moustache groaned as he straightened up. The pain-contorted face slowly turned into an expression full of hatred. "Now I'm going to flatten you, cabrón!" he hissed at Louis in a rage.

The Catalan must have suffered from pathological self-overestimation as he landed two half-hearted karate chops on his angry opponent.

The guard shook himself briefly, then smiled at his enemy with pity. He embraced the small man from the front and lifted him up, squeezing him tighter and tighter. Louis couldn't breathe. He felt incredible pressure on his ribs and his spine felt like a wooden stick that someone was trying to break.

The last thing Louis heard was a terrible crack. Shortly afterwards, his heart stopped beating.

The guard laid the dead Louis Sanchez gently on the ground, as if he were placing a child in a cradle.

Suddenly, he felt a sharp pain in his left ear. The guard, who had just been triumphing over poor Louis, felt immense pain.

A small pocket knife in the hand of a tall blonde woman seemed to have a life of its own. It dug into his ear again and again. Then the two-meter-tall man simply fell forward because he could no longer keep his balance.

As he knelt, Elena Lokova made her final cut, and the small pocket knife that had belonged to Juan Falgas not long ago expertly severed his carotid artery.

Suddenly, the radio in Louis Sanchez's bag crackled again. Elena went over to the dead man lying a few meters away from her, his eyes wide open and his face contorted.

She had a terrible headache and her temples were throbbing wildly.

After she had picked the lock, Juan Falgas threw her against a wall. The Russian woman lost consciousness.

Only after she heard Louis' bones breaking did she come to and manage to leave her dark prison. If she had woken up just five minutes earlier, the man in the torn blue overalls might still be alive.

Elena took the walkie-talkie out of his pocket with her left hand. Almost simultaneously, she closed his eyes with her right hand and crossed herself briefly. That was all she could do for the poor guy.

"Louis, where are you? We're standing outside waiting. Open the damn door!"

Elena flinched for a moment when she heard Jean's voice. She hesitated briefly, then pressed the talk button and spoke.

"Jean, it's me ... Elena. Your two friends are dead, but I didn't kill them. I took care of the security guard. The doctor has my daughter Katharina hostage. I'll explain everything later. Just promise me you won't kill me when I open the door!"

There was silence for a few seconds. Seconds that felt like hours to Elena.

"I promise, now open the door, Elena!"

Elena went to the emergency exit and, after pulling Luca's charred corpse slightly to one side, tried to open the door. The damn thing was stuck. So she braced herself against it with all her might.

At the same time, Henry and Jean were pulling on the other side. Elena thought she could hear them cursing. The pulling and pushing seemed like Sisyphus's labor to the blonde woman. However, the steel door only resisted for a few minutes. But to Elena, it felt like several hours. Because the Russian woman had to expect that a guard would attack her from behind at any moment. Thankfully, the guards didn't notice a thing, and finally the stubborn piece of steel gave way.

Jean and Henry finally entered, and Sarre didn't even glance at Elena, who was bleeding from her forehead. He only looked at her briefly when Henry held a gun out to her. She took the weapon, checked it briefly, and loaded it.

"Mierda," said Henry when he saw the two bodies of Luca and Louis lying there. As Jean passed Louis, he whispered, "Take care, amigo! Peace be with you!"

Somehow, he had grown fond of the small, fat man who always came across as unintentionally funny.

As Henry passed the dead guard's body, he kicked him hard in the side. Not because it would have done any good, but because it was obvious that this bastard had little Louis on his conscience.

The three walked up the long corridor, past several doors behind which they could hear frightened voices. Henry glanced briefly at Jean. "Should we free the Colombians first, Jean?"

Jean waved him off. "That would just cause chaos. Let's take care of the guards first, including that Mengele lookalike. Once the butchers are dead, we'll set the poor bastards free!"

Secretly, Jean was annoyed with himself again for using such language. After all, he couldn't equate the imprisoned people with pigs being led to slaughter.

But he could equate the "hospital staff" and everyone else involved in these terrible deeds with slaughtered pigs.

As they climbed the stairs from the basement of the hospital, Elena and Jean briefly touched arms. It was unintentional, because the staircase was quite narrow.

Jean remembered the tenderness they had exchanged not long ago and quickly dismissed the images from his mind. After all, a fight was imminent and he had to keep a cool head.

When they reached the ground floor, Henry and Jean unconsciously made the same movement. Both grabbed their necks and touched their Judas amulets. Almost as if by telepathy, they glanced at each other briefly, and Jean whispered, "En avant, Henry... One last fight. Saint Jude

Thaddeus, help us!" Henry nodded encouragingly, took his hand off his amulet, and reached for his weapon.

Seconds later, the three were already under fire. A security guard took cover in a corner and fired a 12-gauge shotgun. It was a good thing he had little practice with it.

After a poorly aimed shot, the man was seriously injured in the shoulder. The recoil did its job, and he cursed and whimpered instead of firing a second volley at Jean and his two "brothers in arms."

Instead, he came out of cover and Henry had an easy job with his .357 Magnum. He took a quick aim and shot the guard right in the heart. Henry didn't adhere to any conventions, either in his private life or at work. Especially not when they came from Geneva.

The security guard had a bullet hole about 0.4 inches wide in his chest. But when he fell forward, it was clear that his entire back was missing. Henry had used handmade expanding bullet ammunition, which caused terrible wounds.

Elena, Jean, and Henry didn't have time to catch their breath, though. A security guy rushed toward Jean, yelling, and fired almost his entire magazine while running. All the shots missed. Jean stayed cool, took aim, and fired.

"Click," nothing happened. His SIG Sauer pistol had jammed. The attacker was now four meters in front of Sarre and calmly aimed his weapon at him. He wasn't screaming anymore; instead, the man was now grinning arrogantly at the expert. Jean briefly thought of his patron saint, Judas, and assumed that it was all over.

Then there was a bang and the guard grinned even wider.

However, the grin now resembled that of the Joker, as a bullet fired from the side by Elena spread his lips to at least twice their normal width. In slow motion, Jean saw all the attacker's teeth fly out of his mouth before the man died. There was no question that Elena had just saved Jean's life.

Meanwhile, Henry was in a firefight with two guards. One of his projectiles tore off half a guard's arm. The man died immediately from severe blood loss. Shocked by the sight, the second guard took off.

Just as he ran out of the building and headed for the small gatehouse, his head exploded.

Henry had the rifle, a Blaser R93, also loaded with special expanding bullets.

"No deserting, cabrón," Henry had called after him three seconds earlier.

A security guard who witnessed the whole thing wanted to surrender and raised both arms.

Jean approached him to disarm him.

At the same moment, another guard fired. The fat man who had been hiding behind the information desk the whole time raised his double-barreled shotgun over the counter and was about to fire again. The first shot hit Jean. However, only seven bullets lodged in his left arm. It burned like fire, but Jean was not incapacitated. The second shot hit its target. However, it wasn't Jean, but his blue-uniformed colleague, who had already surrendered.

The poor guy looked at his comrade in disbelief and then fell to the floor, dead.

Before the man could reload, Henry jumped over the information desk and knocked him out with the shoulder stock of his rifle.

The fight with the security guards was over, and Henry tied up the last remaining guard with cable ties.

Jean stood over the unconscious man and shook him hard.

"Where can we find the doctor? Show us the way, you son of a bitch!" The guard slowly regained consciousness and whimpered, "Please don't kill me. I have a wife and children!"

Elena approached the man still kneeling and hit him hard in the face.

"Where is my child, where is my daughter Katharina, where is he hiding her?"

Elena wanted to strike again, but Jean held her back by the sleeve.

"Do you want to knock him unconscious again? Damn it, keep cool! We'll find your little daughter!"

"The chief physician, Dr. Kremer, has his office on the fifth floor," whimpered the security guard. 'The elevator is over there."

"We'll take the stairs so you can work up a sweat, cabrón,' replied Jean. The uniformed man looked down at the floor in shame. Henry grinned broadly, showing his teeth.

Elena reacted irritably to Jean's instruction to wait downstairs. "Forget it, Jean. I'm certainly not going to just wait around twiddling my thumbs. My Katharina is here somewhere. Henry and you can get hold of the doctor. I'm going to look for my daughter and watch out if you see that building contractor Falgas, he mustn't get away."

Said, done. Elena had already disappeared into the stairwell. Henry and Jean exchanged glances and then pushed the man, whose hands were tied, in front of them.

Fifty-five steps later, a security guard stumbled in front of Jean and Henry, his uniform soaked with sweat.

The poor man was completely out of breath and on the verge of a heart attack from climbing the stairs.

"Move, damn it, and walk faster!" Jean snapped at the guard.

"Reminds me of a zombie movie," Henry remarked. "But in slow motion! The zombies in that horror movie ran faster than this damn cabrón!"

Juan Falgas had hidden on the fourth floor and was waiting for his chance. About ten minutes earlier, he had managed to sneak past two guards in the main hall when suddenly a man stood in front of him. The man recognized him and greeted him.

Falgas quickly realized that the guard knew nothing about his imprisonment and still saw him as a "Jefe."

"There are armed intruders down in the basement, and they'll be up here any minute. Call your colleagues and take care of it! I'll inform Dr. Kremer."

The guard nodded briefly and notified his colleagues via his walkie-talkie. Juan Falgas smiled mischievously, certain that these security idiots would now cover his back. This welcome distraction would allow him to walk out of this horror hospital unscathed.

Albeit with two severed heads under his arms. His wife and that insane doctor had to die.

When the shooting started, Juan didn't even look back, but dove up the stairs. He looked for a weapon on the fourth floor because, despite all his pent-up rage, he was well aware that he couldn't kill Mercedes and Eugenio with his bare hands.

If only he had had the chance to grab the guard's gun. But it all happened so fast. He looked for a weapon. Anything to kill or stab them with, but all he found in a small office was a large pair of scissors. Never mind, he would kill them with that.

As he was climbing the stairs to the fifth floor, he heard loud cursing and panting from the stairwell and backed away. He saw two men pushing a visibly exhausted man in front of them. He recognized the guard he had given instructions to a short time ago. He was panting like a hippopotamus in rut. He also recognized the man walking behind him with a determined expression on his face, pushing the other man up the stairs.

"Damn, those who are believed dead live longer," thought Juan. Who in God's name was this damn appraiser?

One floor above Juan, a hysterical nurse named Rita and a determined doctor (to do whatever it takes) had barricaded themselves in his office.

There were actually three of them in the room, which was about twenty square meters in size.

But the third person was neither responsive nor in the best of health. She sat with her head bowed in an office chair, her long black hair hanging in a puddle of brandy, vomit, and blood.

There was no question that Mercedes Falgas was dead. Eugenio had mixed the same poison into her drink that he had used on his former girlfriend in Madrid.

Head nurse Rita didn't trust the dose of poison and wanted to play it safe. Mercedes couldn't move after the poison took effect. She felt like she was in a coma. But she was still aware of the blonde head nurse running her sausage fingers through her well-groomed black hair, literally clawing at her head.

"Like the claws of a vulture," she thought before vomiting.

Rita cursed because the spray had hit her snow-white nurse's uniform.

"Damn bitch!" Disgusted, Rita grabbed the once pretty head and slammed it again and again against the hardwood table.

Behind the face that was being smashed beyond recognition, a brain continued to function for about thirty seconds. Mercedes Falgas saw her life flash before her eyes and, before everything came to an end, she thought once more of the beautiful moments. Among other things, she thought of the Spanish sun, cool drinks, and Jean Sarre, who now couldn't help her anymore.

Eugenio Kremer watched his head nurse with amusement, and after everything was done, he grunted briefly and looked with a broad grin at a large old cabinet standing in the corner of the room.

"Our free pass," he whispered quietly to Rita. Because actually, three hearts were still beating in that office.

Jean Sarre, Henry Batiste, and the still heavily panting security guard with the name Paolo Lesman inspected one room after another on the fifth floor. Before Jean took a look at each room, he first pushed poor Paolo inside.

As a living shield, so to speak. Paolo Lesman was still of value to Henry and Jean, but only as a "bullet trap."

When the three of them stood in front of Eugenio Kremer's locked office, Henry pulled his friend Jean aside.

"Let's blow the door open, Jean. I still have some plastic explosives with me."

Jean looked at his friend in amazement but then nodded in agreement.

"That's right, Henry. I completely forgot about that. But now that all the guards are dead, except for one, we can make as much noise as we want!"

Elena had searched room by room looking for her daughter Katharina and was standing in the hallway on the third floor. There was the so-called playroom, its door open. It was a large, colorful room filled with all kinds of children's toys. In the middle was a ball pit known as a ball pit, consisting of a large wooden box filled with blue, red, and white rubber balls. On the other side was a climbing wall known as a climbing wall that Katharina had once told her about.

The Russian woman sighed briefly and wanted to leave the children's playroom. Then a loud explosion shook the room. All the toys flew through the air and the rubber balls from the ball pit rolled wildly across the floor. They squeaked as they bounced around, and Elena felt that the squeaking sounded more like the panicked cries of children. She covered her ears and wanted to go outside, but the door that had been open before had closed behind her. She was trapped again.

A few grams of plastic explosives did their job. The office door was catapulted into the room, burying Doctor Kremer beneath it. Mercedes Falgas's body was thrown against the ceiling like a puppet. The once beautiful woman then fell onto the large hardwood table where she had previously been killed.

As Jean pushed Paolo through the smoke into the dark room, a wild fury ran towards them. Rita's once blonde hair was now burnt black and her neat nurse's uniform hung in tatters.

Paolo Lesman didn't stand a chance. Head nurse Rita, who now resembled a crazed witch, jumped at the security guard, screaming hysterically, and stabbed him in the chest with a long kitchen knife, killing him.

Henry, who was standing a meter behind Jean, didn't hesitate.

Before Rita could stab Jean, he blew half her head off with his .357 Magnum.

As if in a trance and deafened by the shot, Jean walked toward the door in the middle of the room. Only the head of Dr. Eugenio Kremer was visible beneath the blown-away section.

The doctor reminded Jean of a carp gasping for air on dry land, its mouth open for a long time and then closing again briefly. Following an inner impulse, he took one of the two silver coins from his pocket and roughly stuck it in his mouth. Eugenio wanted to spit it out, but in the end he didn't have the strength.

With loud curses, Henry and Jean lifted the heavy door together. As soon as Eugenio was free, he crawled to his desk, pulled himself up by the legs and sat down awkwardly in his oversized executive chair.

"Where is this Falgas?" Jean shouted at him, but the doctor didn't seem to understand him and instead rubbed his ears frantically.

Then he slowly stood up, staggered to a cabinet, and opened a side door.

Henry had his revolver pointed at him the whole time. But he instinctively lowered the gun when a little girl appeared.

"Katharina?" Henry and Jean looked at the girl with relief.

Even Dr. Eugenio Kremer smiled. But when the child took a few steps toward Jean, the doctor abruptly pulled her back toward him. Suddenly, he held a scalpel to Elena's daughter's throat.

Henry pointed his gun at the surgeon again.

"Hijo de puta, son of a bitch! Don't you dare hurt that girl!" Jean was furious, but he also knew that the doctor had the upper hand with his little hostage.

"Don't make me kill the child," Eugenio hissed. "If you two don't follow me, I'll let her go as soon as I'm safe. But if you cause me any trouble, I'll slit the child's throat, and believe me, I won't feel a thing!"

Henry and Jean looked at him in disgust. But they also knew that he had taken them by surprise with this move, and they stood rooted to the spot.

The doctor pushed Katharina past them and, as he left the room, almost stepped on his former head nurse.

When he glanced down and saw the charred and almost headless Rita, the corners of his mouth twitched. But this nervous movement was over in a split second. Completely devoid of empathy, he picked up Elena's daughter and ran to the stairwell.

One floor below, Juan Falgas waited for his chance. When he heard heavy footsteps on the stairs, he slowly crept closer so he could stab with his scissors.

Like a toy clown trying to jump out of a joke box with a spring. Juan's tension was just as great.

At the last moment, he realized it was Kremer. Eugenio Kremer, who was carrying something on his back. Juan wanted to let him pass and then stab him from behind. But when he saw that Eugenio was carrying a little girl on his back, he hesitated and couldn't do it.

Eugenio ran past him, panting, with a crying child in his arms. Juan thought for a moment and then finally ran after him.

Meanwhile, one floor below, the door to the playroom opened.

Elena had once again managed to pick the lock with her small pocket knife.

As soon as the door was half open, the rubber balls from the ball pit rolled out. Elena had the feeling that the balls were literally jostling to enjoy their new freedom.

They rolled toward the stairwell and seemed to be drawn by some tremendous force. Juan Falgas, who was perhaps ten meters behind Eugenio and Katharina, was just passing the third floor when a bunch of bouncing balls pushed their way in front of his feet.

White, blue, and red ones gathered in front of him.

Juan was literally attacked by them and couldn't get out of the way.

"Mierda, damn it," he thought as he lost his balance, tumbled down the stairs, and fell down the staircase. The long scissors rammed into his right thigh, and when he, or rather his skull, was abruptly stopped by the wall on the second floor, he lost consciousness.

Elena ran after him. Like an invisible force, the many rubber balls moved away from her feet so that the tall blonde woman wouldn't trip. Somehow, the whole scene was reminiscent of Moses parting the sea and leading his Israelites to safety with dry feet, while their Egyptian pursuers drowned in the floods.

Doctor Eugenio Kremer had meanwhile left the main building. The doctor was on his way to the illuminated parking lot. It was still dark, and Elena's little daughter Katharina was sitting on his back like a clinging monkey, crying her eyes out.

The doctor wondered why he should bother with this unnecessary burden. Empathy was foreign to him anyway, and in the current situation, Katharina was more of a risk to him.

He didn't like animals or children. In fact, he didn't even like people. He loved only three things: money, food, and himself!

The closeness he had built up with Elena's daughter over time had been nothing more than a big charade.

Katharina trusted him because children are easily influenced and couldn't see the monster behind his small button eyes.

He briefly considered simply letting Katharina go. However, two things stood in the way of this.

Firstly, he wanted to take revenge on Elena, and secondly, the child shouldn't be able to tell anyone what vehicle he was driving or which direction he was heading in.

"Now, Katharina, my little one, stop crying," he said to the girl and took her off his shoulders.

Eugenio stood the child in front of him and stroked her hair tenderly.

When the girl looked at him briefly, he smiled and turned her around 180 degrees.

"There, Kathi, look at the river, we're waiting here for your mom! Do you see the osprey back there?"

Eugenio knew that Elena's daughter liked to draw eagles and all kinds of animals, and tried to distract her with this. But the question itself was pointless, as it was difficult to see anything in the darkness.

With one hand, he held the little girl by the shoulders from behind, and with the other, he searched his smeared smock for a tool with which he could "quickly and painlessly" dispose of his little witness. His always sharp scalpel.

When he finally found it, he wanted to simply draw it across the thin child's neck with an elegant swing. "You'll see your mother soon," whispered Eugenio, not wanting to waste any more time. Then something hard hit him in the back. He felt a blow to the back of his knees and fell to the ground.

A figure covered in seaweed, moss, and clay had stopped him from killing his sixty-fifth child with a square log.

Eugenio shuddered violently and slowly got back to his feet. His scalpel had pierced his right hand during the fall. But he was so terrified of the figure, which looked like the monster from the swamp, that he simply pulled it out and waved it wildly.

The figure wanted to follow him and kill him with the square timber, but little Katharina grabbed his moss-green hand.

"Let him go! Take me to my mommy!

Katharina suddenly spoke calmly and firmly, and her handshake seemed demanding.

Somehow, this handshake reminded the creepy-looking man of the hand that pulled him out of the raging river just before he drowned.

In that moment, all the hatred fell away from him and he walked hand in hand with the little girl back to the hospital.

Eugenio looked after them in bewilderment, laughed loudly, got into a car, and drove away.

On the one hand, Kremer rejoiced that he had been able to escape, but on the other hand, he had a strange metallic taste in his mouth and was suffering from unpleasant, persistent belching.

Juan Falgas was plagued by terrible headaches. His temples were throbbing wildly and his right leg was bleeding. As if through a cloudy veil, he noticed Elena grabbing him by the shoulders. Shortly afterwards, Jean and Henry joined them.

When the Russian woman heard from Sarre that Dr. Kremer had taken her daughter hostage, she wasted no time and rushed down the stairs.

She ran past the information desk, past the bodies of the security guards, and slipped on a large pool of blood. As she got up again, cursing, her breath caught in her throat.

A moss-green apparition was just walking through the main entrance of the hospital. The worst part was that this creepy mixture of a tree and a crocodile was standing next to her little daughter.

She pulled out her gun and aimed it at him.

"Don't shoot, don't shoot! It's me, it's me ... Pascal!"

At that moment, Katharina came running toward them.

"Mommy, Mommy!" Katharina slid across the blood-stained floor straight into her mother's arms, who hugged her tightly.

After Elena had made sure that her daughter was unharmed, she turned to Pascal.

"Damn it, Pascal, what happened to you? Did you come back from the dead? Thank you for bringing my daughter back. Thank you a thousand times!"

Pascal took a towel that someone had left on a visitor's chair and at least wiped his face clean.

"De nada, no problem, but I let my brother's killer get away and I don't understand why. As long as that sadistic Satan isn't dead, I won't rest!" Tears ran down Pascal's face, but he immediately wiped them away with the towel. He just didn't want the tall blonde woman to see.

He slowly regained control of his trembling voice and tried to appear confident.

Seconds later, Jean and Henry came around the corner. They were pushing Juan Falgas, who was limping noticeably, noisily in front of them.

When Jean recognized who was staring at him, he actually started laughing out loud.

"Hahahaha... hey... hola Loco, I can't believe it, the river spat you out again. Look at him, Henry. That clumsy Pascal must have seven lives!"

Henry smiled broadly, threw the miserable Falgas to the ground, and ran towards Pascal to give him a friendly hug.

Henry squeezed him so hard that the man from Figueres almost couldn't breathe.

However, Jean and Henry's faces quickly darkened when Pascal told them that Doctor Kremer had escaped.

Then Jean turned to Elena. "You and your daughter had better get in your car right now. Get out of here! I'll call Detective Inspector Ruiz when we're done with this piece of shit!" He pointed to Juan Falgas, who was cowering on the ground.

Henry reached into his pocket and handed Elena a key.

"Drive straight to Barcelona and make yourselves comfortable in my apartment. As soon as we've sorted everything out here, we'll join you."

Elena nodded gratefully to Henry. After the two had discussed where and how, she took her little Katharina by the hand and left.

Mother and daughter left the Pedro Leon Hospital without looking back.

CHAPTER 17: *Juanito has to bleed*

It was still dark and the full moon was hidden behind the clouds when Falgas was tied to an old pine tree by Jean. Secured with cable ties and rope and gagged with a torn shirt, there was nothing left of the former construction magnate. The entrepreneur had lost all his elegance and chic, and even his gold wristwatch now looked somehow surreal on him. In these lighting conditions, the yellow gold of the Breitling couldn't show off its beauty. But even if it had shone like the sun, none of the men showed any interest in Juan's luxury watch. Not even the thief from Figueres.

Henry and Pascal waited about twenty meters away, watching the goings-on with interest but full of thoughts of revenge.

Then Jean briefly removed the gag from the prisoner's mouth, whereupon the latter began to curse loudly.

"Vosotros sois Hijos de Putas, you sons of whores, untie me so I can rip your fucking skulls off. I'll rip your heads off and shit down your throats!"

He didn't get any further, because Jean suddenly and forcefully stuck a silver coin in his mouth and gagged him again before he could spit it out.

What happened next seemed like a drug trip to Jean and the other men in the small forest clearing.

The moon was now shining much brighter, and Jean, Pascal, and Henry were unable to move. Jean wasn't the only one who felt like he had been turned into a pillar of salt. The three men felt like they were in a bad dream when suddenly a large gray wolf stepped out of the shadows of the trees.

The predator moved purposefully toward the terrified Juan Falgas.

Very slowly and growling deeply, Master Isegrim first took a sniff, then approached the bound Juan to sniff extensively at his bleeding leg wound.

Juan opened his eyes wide in disgust and tried to kick the wolf, but he felt that it wasn't just the ropes that were holding him back. The tree was holding him fast. This cursed old pine tree was literally sucking him in. So strongly that he couldn't move an inch.

Baring its teeth and growling, the animal suddenly reared up, bit down, and dragged the battered man along.

But Juan Falgas had the feeling that the wolf didn't want to kill him right away.

This animal, scientifically known as "Canis Lupus," was torturing him and taking its time doing so.

The large, gray predator bit again and again. With just one bite to Juan's throat, it could have ended the former entrepreneur's life.

But that's not what it did. Instead, it concentrated on his arms and legs.

Then suddenly, the large wolf turned to Jean Sarre, moved around the frozen man, and sat down demonstratively next to him.

The large brown eyes suddenly radiated a warmth that reminded Jean of his killed dog.

With its mouth covered in blood, the wolf gently licked Jean's hand and looked him in the eyes.

At that moment, Jean recognized his Arthos behind the wolf's eyes. He was then able to move again briefly. He knelt down next to Isegrim and stroked his head tenderly. The predator briefly raised his lips and growled softly, but Jean felt that the touch was good for both of them.

Finally, he was able to say goodbye to his friend Arthos, who had been torn to pieces in the bomb attack.

Jean Sarre slowly got up again, smiling. The large, gray predator trotted away and disappeared into the shadows of the Pyrenean forest.

Henry and Pascal were still unable to move. They stood rooted to the spot when, unexpectedly, a herd of wild boars appeared in the clearing. Several sows and their piglets romped around the old pine tree and looked more or less puzzled at the bound Juan. At the edge of the clearing, a lead sow watched over her herd. The wild boar grunted as it surveyed the whole scene.

One small piglet became curious. It sniffed the contractor's fresh wounds and bit his leg courageously. Juan tried to scream, but the gag muffled his cry of pain to a soft sigh.

Suddenly, a loud crackling and snorting sound could be heard in the undergrowth about two hundred yards away. The lead sow bellowed briefly.

Immediately, the entire herd of wild boars ran in the opposite direction.

The pigs ran in a panic from the moonlit clearing and sought shelter in the darkness of the forest.

Seconds later, a monstrous wild boar emerged from the adjacent hedges. Jean had never seen such a large wild boar before.

But both he and Pascal probably remembered the huge tracks they had discovered in the mud a short time earlier.

Snorting wildly, the wild boar moved toward the large pine tree, which now resembled a torture stake.

While Jean was still unconsciously wondering how much this creature might weigh, the slaughter began. This pig took no prisoners.

It stamped toward Juan, grunting loudly, and immediately lunged at him.

With its razor-sharp tusks, at least eight inches long, it first bit off the defenseless man's arms and legs.

The wild boar fell into such a blood frenzy that it ripped open Juan's lower abdomen to tear at his intestines. The intestines hung out like a long snake, and the wild pig simply pulled on them.

The old pine tree creaked under the attacks and finally released Señor Falgas. The ropes came loose, or perhaps they were simply bitten through. In any case, Juan, who was still alive and consisted only of his head and torso, fell from the tree onto the soft forest floor.

The fall also loosened the gag in Falgas' mouth, and Jean and his two companions heard the most bone-shaking screams of pain they had ever heard in their lives.

The huge boar was not in the least disturbed by the screams. He simply dragged the dying man behind him and disappeared as loudly and snorting as he had come. Only a long trail of blood leading into the darkness remained as a reminder of the former construction magnate. Then there was dead silence.

The full moon regained its original brightness, and Jean, Henry, and Pascal were able to move again and talk to each other.

"Mierda, what the hell was that!" Pascal almost shouted, looking at Henry and Jean in horror.

The three men looked at each other in disbelief. When Pascal tried to pick up a silver coin lying on the forest floor, Jean motioned for him to leave it alone.

At the same time, the men heard loud sirens in the distance. Inspector Carlos Ruiz arrived, late as always, but Jean now knew that the prisoners would finally be freed.

In any case, Henry, Pascal, and he would not have to set foot in that horror hospital again, and that was a good thing.

About two months later, a relaxed Jean Sarre was sitting at a kitchen table reading a Catalan newspaper. It wasn't easy, because a small black-brown puppy kept demanding his attention. The German hunting terrier was only ten weeks old and quite exhausting. However, Jean had fallen head over heels in love with little "Lucy." Of course, he was still mourning his male dog Arthos, but as soon as sadness overwhelmed him, Lucy was there to distract him. The little terrier, who reminded Jean of a miniature Doberman, was harder to control than a bag of fleas.

"Can you make me a sandwich for school, please?" Katharina had quietly crept up to him and smiled at him with wide eyes.

"Sure, sweetie, I'll do that for you!" Jean was about to get up when a newspaper article caught his eye.

"The hospital of horror ... Inspector Carlos Ruiz uncovers large-scale organ trafficking ... He freed hundreds of prisoners from the clutches of the organ mafia ... Several masterminds are still on the run... Inspector Ruiz is being promoted ..."

The newspaper article even speculated that Carlos Ruiz might deserve the Order of the Golden Fleece. This order is the highest honor that the Spanish royal family can bestow.

Jean grinned. This lazy cop was just responding to his text message after Henry, Pascal, and he had saved the day.

Not to mention Elena. Where was she, anyway?

Oh yes, she was now managing several of Henry's clubs and was already out early in the morning.

Jean wasn't entirely happy with this situation, but here in Barcelona, life had to go on somehow.

Henry had even chartered a small yacht for them for the coming weekend. Katharina, in particular, couldn't talk about anything else.

Thankfully, the girl had recovered somewhat from the horrors of the Pyrenees hospital and was now even able to sleep in her own bed. However, the night light had to be on and the bedroom door had to be left slightly open. Little Lucy, who was already wide awake, also gave the girl an extra feeling of security.

Katharina would immediately panic in a pitch-dark room, perhaps because of the closet where Eugenio had locked the little girl up for a long time.

Just as Jean was thinking about that sadistic bastard again, his smartphone rang.

Unknown caller ... Jean thought briefly about whether he should answer the call, but then decided to do so.

Meanwhile, Katharina was still waiting for her packed lunch.

"Sarre!" At first, he heard nothing on the other end, then a brief rustling sound, followed by something that sounded like church bells.

"Hola, cabrón ... How are Elena, the little one, and you, my friend?"

Jean smiled and put the bread knife down for a moment.

"Pascal, pendejo... damn good to hear you. Are you in jail again? Where are you calling from?"

The ringing grew louder.

"No, no, mi amigo. I've got a good job in Cadaqués! I'm a sexton at the Eglesia de Santa Maria now. I don't earn much, but I have everything I need and I don't feel like drinking or doing drugs anymore!"

"Hey, from Saul to Paul, congratulations, Pascal!"

Jean couldn't help thinking of Saint Jude and unconsciously touched his amulet. The patron saint of hopeless cases had also done a good job with Pascal.

Pascal said that an old woman had got him the job, but he couldn't shake the feeling that he knew this grandmotherly figure from another life.

Jean smiled briefly, but then dark thoughts took over again.

"Have you heard anything about your brother's murderer, Pascal?"

"Yes and no," replied the Catalan after a short pause.

"A few days ago, I was once again filled with hatred and thoughts of revenge. I racked my brains and was on the verge of giving up everything here and searching for that miserable murderer, if necessary to the ends of the earth. But then that old woman came up to me again, put her hand on my shoulder and whispered something quietly in my ear."

"That doctor will get his just punishment, the old woman said." There was another long pause on the phone.

"Hey Jean, how could she know that? How the hell could that abuela know what I was thinking?"

Jean took a deep breath, but wasn't really surprised.

"Do you know the old woman's name, Pascal? Do you know her name?"

It took a moment for the Catalan to answer.

"Maria," Pascal replied.

Jean wasn't really surprised. He had guessed it. Although probably millions of women had that name.

"This Maria also told me that I should buy a national newspaper next week. In it, I would find an article that would restore my inner peace permanently. Crazy, isn't it?"

"What isn't crazy in this world, Pascal! Anyway, I'm glad you're okay. Take care of yourself, stay clean, and let's talk again soon.

It's best if you call me again next week. Take care, see you then!"

"Adiós, mi amigo, see you next week."

" Adiós, cabrón, hasta luego."

Pascal ended the call, and after Jean hung up too, he could finally finish making Katharina's lunch.

As the girl was on her way to school, Jean stood on the small balcony to let his thoughts wander while smoking a cigarette. In the distance, he could see the Sagrada Familia. It was probably the most famous Roman Catholic basilica and a tourist attraction in Barcelona. It was still unfinished, even though construction had begun in 1882. Jean thought of its architect, Antonio Gaudi, and how he had lost his life. The architect had been hit by a tram on his way to work. Because Gaudi looked more like a beggar due to his unkempt appearance and did not carry any identification, he was not taken to a hospital for the poor until several hours later. Three days later, his friends found him and had him transferred. It was too late; he died that same day.

"No first aid because the police thought he was a useless bum. Probably untreated broken bones and internal bleeding."

"Tragic," thought Jean, taking a deep breath.

CHAPTER 18: *far away but not safe yet*

Sweaty, "El Medico" placed the scalpel above the pubic bone. It was important not to cut too deep so as not to damage the goods.

He carefully moved the blade toward the sternum and got the rib spreader ready.

Large fruit flies buzzed frantically around him. As soon as he stopped cutting, they settled down to lay their eggs on the lifeless female body.

The small, windowless room now reeked of death and rotting flesh.

Eugenio gradually pulled small bags out of the corpse.

Bags containing a snow-white powder.

He carefully rubbed the baggies clean, taking great care not to tear any of them. After all, every bag that burst was a huge loss. It didn't matter that the drug courier who had smuggled the narcotics in his body was dead.

Of course, the cartel was only interested in profit. The lives of these people were worth nothing to the drug mafia.

After Dr. Eugenio Kremer had done his job, he waved to a small camera standing in the corner. This way, his employers knew that he had fulfilled his duty and could, of course, monitor him. Mutual trust was rather unusual in this business.

He held the pouches up to the camera one by one and then put them in an inconspicuous shopping bag. Then he went to the door, which opened slowly.

Two cartel soldiers were waiting outside, still talking loudly about some women.

Eugenio gave the bag to one of them, said a quick goodbye, and then walked over to an old pickup truck where a man was already waiting for him.

"Well, done for today, Doctore?"

The driver grinned smugly at Eugenio, waiting for a response, but in vain.

Kremer was lost in thought on the way to his hotel.

He thought wistfully of Spain, of his position as chief physician at the hospital in Vidasacra, and not least of his head nurse Rita, whose devoted manner he apparently missed.

"It's only when you lose something that you realize its true value," mused the doctor.

Since he had been working here in the Colombian back country, he had been terribly homesick, and even alcohol and sweets could not alleviate his sadness.

The painkillers he swallowed all day long only exacerbated his stomach problems. He still had that persistent belching, and the metallic taste in his mouth would not go away.

When they arrived at the small, musty hotel, the driver braked abruptly on the dusty road and Eugenio cursed because the inertia almost catapulted him against the windshield. They almost ran over a small dog. The black-brown mutt suddenly stood in the middle of the road. Dr. Kremer got out awkwardly and tried to chase the dog away with all his might. The animal didn't find this funny at all and immediately sank its teeth into Eugenio's right calf.

When the driver also got out, the street dog finally let go of Eugenio and ran away barking.

"You don't like animals, do you?" The man shook his head and looked at Eugenio with pity.

The doctor was still standing there with his pants torn when the rusty pickup truck drove off again.

"Mierda, now I'll have to use the iodine ointment again," he thought as he entered the dilapidated hotel.

Just a few days ago, a small cat had literally attacked him and scratched him badly.

He didn't like animals, but they had never reacted so aggressively towards him before. As soon as he entered the room, he immediately reached for the cognac bottle to wash away the metallic taste.

Then he went to a small bedside table next to a rickety bed and looked for his current favorite food. No sooner had he opened the drawer than a packet of his favorite chocolate bars fell at his feet.

The bedside table was overflowing with his sweets, but just like the brandy, they didn't mask his bad breath.

Suddenly, he realized that he was actually exhausted, and let himself fall backwards onto the yellowed mattress. He lay on the bed with at least fifteen chocolate bars next to him and didn't fall asleep until he had eaten them all.

It wasn't long before his nightmares came back. They usually started with him lying on the operating table.

The people he had tortured and ultimately killed surrounded him and held him down.

Children, mothers, old and young men. Each of them held a scalpel in their hand and laughed as they cut pieces of flesh from his body. He screamed in pain, but they didn't let up. They continued cutting relentlessly.

The dream always ended with an old woman suddenly appearing.

She completed his martyrdom by driving her long, bony fingers into his chest.

Then she took something out of him. An almost black heart that was still beating and pulsing. She held it high in the air above him and the people around him roared. The old woman smiled meaningfully at him. Then she simply tore his heart apart and threw it to his former victims, who ate it while screaming hysterically.

After this dream sequence, he always woke up, reached for the cognac bottle, and polished off one of his beloved chocolate bars. Today, he wanted to numb himself with chocolate again, but since he could only feel empty, torn wrappers around him, he was forced to get up.

Eugenio rolled heavily out of bed and pulled open the bedside table drawer. He took out a new packet when he noticed an ant frantically trying to escape from the drawer.

Eugenio didn't need a second eater, so he made short work of it and killed it with his slipper.

The ant had seemed quite large to him, and its remains were now probably under the sole of his slipper.

Never mind, he would let the property management know tomorrow. After all, vermin, insects, and anything that crawls and flies had to be reported. Then the hotel owners would just have to pay for an exterminator.

The nightmare hadn't helped Eugenio relax, and after the incident with the ant, he felt even more tired than before.

So he flopped back onto his bed and devoured three more chocolate bars before falling asleep again.

Shortly after reaching the REM phase, his very own nightmare began all over again.

Once again, he was lying on the operating table, surrounded by his former patients. Once again, they held him down and began to cut him.

Only this time, he felt the agony as if it were real.

Every single cut felt indescribably painful. It hurt so much that he had to wake up.

When he woke up, he felt like a cardboard dummy at a shooting range. It felt as if he had been caught in a hail of bullets. Crossfire from all directions.

He opened his eyes and saw himself covered with ants.

These South American giant ants, or "Paraponera clavata" in scientific terms, are also called "bullet ants" because their sting is equivalent to a gunshot wound on the pain scale.

Eugenio wanted to scream at the top of his lungs, but only a tortured rattle escaped his lips. The insects bit and stung him over and over again.

He hoped he was dreaming. But with every single wound inflicted, he realized he was in reality.

After several hours of absolute torture, a single ant took pity on him. It wandered over his lips, crawled into his jaw, which was torn open from the pain, deep into his throat, and bit him several times.

Only a few minutes later, Dr. Eugenio Kremer suffocated, with a crushed chocolate bar in his right hand and a silver coin on his swollen tongue.

No human being or animal would mourn him in any way.

CHAPTER 19: *It'll be alright (epilogue)*

Pascal was just connecting the old pressure washer to clean the dirty church wall. This work was also one of his new tasks. The "Eglesia de Santa Maria" was a popular tourist attraction in Cadaqués, and Pascal had the impression that almost everyone leaned against the church wall to take souvenir photos.

Well, the view of the picturesque bay with its many colorful ships and boats was fantastic, after all.

The compressor had just started up loudly when the wind blew a crumpled newspaper in his direction.

"Damn Tramuntana!" Pascal put the steam jet's spray lance aside for a moment, picked up the newspaper, and smoothed it out a little.

His attention was immediately drawn to an article that made his pulse race.

"Spanish surgeon killed by giant ants!" Were sweets left out the cause of the insect attack? ... Blah, blah, blah ... Maybe it was a form of suicide?

Pascal read the article and then laughed out loud.

So loud that even the running compressor couldn't compete with him in terms of volume.

It was a liberating laugh, a laugh that lifted a heavy burden from his soul. ***

Thanks for reading, and hope you enjoyed it.
OJP (June 2025)

A little self-promotion

Book description:

8 short stories about 8 nightmares! Classic and dystopian horror stories.

From witches, werewolves, vampires, and voodoo to crazy robots, self-driving cars, and malicious fitness trackers!

a short excerpt:

... Two hours later, he heard Vivaldi's "Four Seasons," and when the violins began to play »summer«, his maltreated index finger suddenly began to ache. It burned and throbbed wildly. Annoyed, George got up from the sofa, tore off the bandage, and went straight to the bathroom to hold his hand under cold water. Since the cool water wet provided little relief, he took an ice pack out of the freezer and wrapped it around his finger. Before doing so, he looked at the bite mark, but apart from a small scratch, he couldn't really see anything.

He flinched suddenly. What was that noise outside out there, and why the hell did he care about the discussions of the people living in the house across the street? Then he heard a short rustling sound ... followed by a slight squeak. When he got up and peered out the window, he saw that about a hundred meters away a small rat was rummaging around a discarded garbage bag. Damn, he didn't even have his glasses on, how could it be that he could suddenly see so clearly and literally hear the grass grow? It took a few minutes for George to realize what was happening to him, but he couldn't explain it. The pain he had just been feeling was blown away. He felt better than he had in a long time. George suddenly had a ravenous appetite. It wasn't just the craving for meat that overcame him, but rather the craving for the life itself ...

Coming soon for my English-speaking friends.

Peace, freedom, love, and keep on rockin'! OJP